www.bearigo.com

Venus: Guardian of the Realm'

Authors: Daniel Smart & Elisangela Bearigo

ISBN: 979-8-89496-490-4 (Ebook)

ISBN: 979-8-89496-499-7 (Paperback)

This book, Venus: Guardian of the Realm, is a work of fiction. Unless otherwise indicated, all names, characters, businesses, places, events, and incidents in this book are either the product of the authors' imagination or used in a fictitious manner. Any resemblance to actual persons, living or dead, or actual events is purely coincidental.

Although the authors and publisher have made every effort to ensure that the information in this book was correct at press time, they do not assume and hereby disclaim any liability to any party for any loss, damage, or disruption caused by errors or omissions, whether such errors or omissions result from negligence, accident, or any other cause.

Copyright Owner: Daniel Smart and Elisangela Bearigo

Copyright © 2024 Daniel Smart and Elisangela Bearigo

First Printing Edition 2024

Bearigo International LLP

71-75 Shelton Street

Covent Garden

London

WC2H 9JQ

UNITED KINGDOM

www.bearigo.com

CONTENTS

DEDICATION

To Venus, our French Bulldog, whose spirit and bravery have inspired every page of this story. When we began writing this book, Venus was battling through a stroke and had lost an eye, casting uncertainty over her future. Her strength during those challenging times became a beacon of hope for us.

Venus has been more than a companion; she has been a guiding light, sitting by our side as we wove this tale of magic and heroism. Her presence infused our writing with a unique sense of purpose and wonder. As you read these pages, know that this book is not just a work of fiction but a heartfelt tribute to her enduring spirit.

We hope that as you journey through this magical world, you will fall in love with Venus, just as we have. She is a hero in every sense of the word, believing in magic with a heart full of courage. Whether the world we've created is real or a flight of imagination is for you to decide. But remember, in our hearts, Venus is a true star—shining brightly in every chapter.

Chapter 1 – 'Unexpected Guidance'

The bustling metropolis of Evergreen City was a fusion of modern technology and ancient magic, sadly long forgotten. Sleek trams glided down tree-lined streets, the hum of their engines harmonizing with the quiet whispers of enchantments. The air was thick with the scents of both nature and magic—hints of fresh blooms mingling with the heady fragrance of mystical herbs—still amidst the urban vibrancy.

Nestled close by within the enchanted woods, Evelyn's charming cottage stood tall and proud. The thatched roof was adorned with vibrant flowers, and the walls were painted in warm hues that seemed to radiate magic. The townsfolk whispered of the eccentric woman who lived within its walls, known for her kind heart and powerful herbal potions. But what truly set her apart was her deep connection to the natural world. With every breath she took, she could feel the energy of the forest coursing through her veins. Her constant companion, a small French Bulldog named Venus, bounded beside her with endless energy and curiosity, stealing the hearts of all who crossed their path.

It was the first Monday of spring, and the serene aura of the cottage was violently ruptured by Evelyn's frantic and erratic movements. Venus, usually content on her cushion by the window, now lay unnaturally motionless with shallow, ragged breaths. Evelyn's heart thudded with terror as she dropped to her knees beside her cherished companion, whispering desperate words of comfort in a futile attempt to ease her suffering.

Evelyn's heart broke as she watched Venus lying motionless, a single tear escaping her eye. She whispered a plea to the goddess, hoping for a miracle in this desperate moment. But when no improvement was seen, Evelyn realized she needed assistance beyond her homemade remedies and herbal concoctions stacked on her kitchen shelves.

Urgently, she bundled Venus into a soft blanket and rushed out of the cottage, determined to seek aid from the local vet. The journey seemed endless, every minute amplifying her anxiety. Finally, she arrived at the small clinic and burst through the doors, breathless and anxious.

Dr. Larson, the town's kind-hearted veterinarian, greeted her with a concerned expression as she stumbled into the examination room. "Evelyn, what's wrong?"

"It's Venus," Evelyn choked out, her voice breaking with emotion. "She's very sick. Please, help her."

With gentle hands, Dr. Larson took Venus from Evelyn's arms and began a thorough examination. Evelyn paced nervously, her heart aching with worry for her beloved companion. After what felt like hours, Dr. Larson finally looked up, his expression grave.

"Evelyn, I'm afraid Venus has had a stroke," he said softly. "Her left eye is paralyzed, and it's beyond saving. We'll need to remove it to prevent further complications."

Evelyn felt her world shatter at those words. "A stroke? How could this happen?" she asked in disbelief.

"It's rare but not unheard of," Dr. Larson explained gently. "The most important thing now is to ensure she recovers fully and learns to adapt without her eye. With your love and care, I believe she can pull through."

Tears streamed down Evelyn's face as she nodded, willing to do whatever it takes to save her precious Venus. As they prepared for surgery, Evelyn stayed by Venus's side, whispering soothing words and promising to be there when she woke up.

As the hours ticked by, Evelyn's mind raced with worry and fear. But finally, Dr. Larson emerged from the operating room, his expression calm. "The surgery was a success. Venus is resting now. She's a fighter."

Evelyn let out a sigh of relief and gratitude. "Thank you, Dr. Larson. Thank you so much."

"You can see her now," he said, leading Evelyn to a small recovery area where Venus lay, still and peaceful.

Evelyn approached her beloved pet, gently caressing her fur and whispering words of love and encouragement. She knew this was just the beginning of Venus's long road to recovery, but she vowed to do everything in her power to help her heal.

She thanked Dr. Larson once again before wrapping Venus in the soft, warm blanket, carrying her with tender care back to their cozy cottage. As they left the clinic, Evelyn felt a chill in the air that was not entirely due to the weather. She looked down at the bundled form of Venus in her arms, a knot of anxiety forming in her chest.

Over the next five days, Evelyn tended to Venus with unwavering devotion. She prepared carefully measured doses of medications prescribed by Dr. Larson and nourishing meals that she spoon-fed to her weak companion. She cleaned her wound daily with gentle precision, ensuring it remained free from infection.

Despite her tireless efforts, Venus's recovery was slow and filled with struggle. The once-spirited dog could barely move without assistance, each attempt resulting in a heart-wrenching fall. Her remaining eye reflected an almost human-like sadness, stirring a deep-rooted fear within Evelyn's heart.

As the dim light of Saturday morning crept through the windows, six long days since Venus's operation, Evelyn could feel a sense of desperation settling in. Despite her best efforts, Venus's condition had not improved. She lay on the hard floor, barely moving and showing no signs of improvement. As Evelyn surveyed the small cottage, she realized that their food supplies were dangerously low. Even the milk for her morning coffee had run dry. With a heavy heart, she knew she had to leave the comfort of the cottage and tend to their needs.

Reluctantly, Evelyn stepped out into the crisp morning air, leaving Venus behind. She whispered to her beloved companion, "I won't let you go. I'll find a way to help you." The weight of her promise hung heavily on her shoulders as she made her way to the village market. The sun was just beginning to rise over the horizon, casting a warm glow over the sleepy streets. But for Evelyn, there was no warmth or comfort in this peaceful scene—only worry and determination to find a solution for Venus's ailment.

Evelyn navigated through the bustling square, where nearly everyone around her walked with their heads down, engrossed in their mobile phones. The crowd moved with purpose, yet they were living in a virtual world, disconnected from the reality around them. People rudely bumped into each other, muttering apologies without looking up. Even when buying goods from the stall holders, their interactions were curt and dismissive, the information on their screens more important than the human connection in front of them. In the midst of this sea of distraction, Beatrice emerged, her presence a stark contrast to the detached crowd. Despite not being a young woman, Beatrice exuded an unending energy that could rival any youth. Her true age was impossible to determine; she could have been anywhere between forty and seventy years old. Her spirit remained vibrant and untouched by the passing of time, combining wisdom from countless experiences with a contagious enthusiasm.

This gave her a timeless quality, making it impossible to pinpoint her in a specific stage of life.

Her appearance was as eccentric as her reputation suggested. She boasted an abundant mane of silver hair cascading down to her shoulders in loose curls, twinkling under the sun as if kissed by the morning dew. It framed her face beautifully, accentuating her high cheekbones that were dusted with a roseate blush, a sign of the early morning chill. Her eyes were vivacious and bright, a striking blue that mirrored a tempestuous sea yet carried an inexplicable calmness.

Her physique was lean yet sturdy, like a seasoned traveler who had treaded uncountable miles. Each movement seemed like a dance, fluid and graceful, carrying an aura of mesmerizing comfort around her. There was a certain agility about her, not the kind born from youth but crafted out of years of adventure and exploration. Her posture was impeccable, each step measured with an unspoken confidence that subtly commanded attention.

She was dressed in an array of colors that could rival the most vibrant sunrise. Multiple layers of exotic fabrics swaddled her figure; skirts of emerald green, sapphire blue, and amethyst purple, a blouse of bright yellow with intricate floral embroidery that showcased her artistic flair. Her jewelry jingled with each step she took—a symphony of metal and glass—bangles of silver and turquoise, an amulet around her neck adorned with sacred symbols, all carrying tales from lands afar.

It's safe to say that Beatrice was the standout amongst the crowd, and Evelyn should have noticed her earlier. However, her thoughts were consumed with concern for Venus.

"Evelyn!" Beatrice called, her voice rich and embracing like a warm mug of cocoa on a cold night. But there was no returning smile from Evelyn.

"Beatrice," Evelyn responded with a slight nod. Her eyes, usually sparkling like topaz under sunlight, reflected a dull glimmer of worry.

"What's wrong, dear?" Beatrice asked, concern lining her words as she took in the sight of Evelyn's haggard face.

"It's Venus," Evelyn finally admitted, looking back at Beatrice with saddened eyes that held barely concealed despair. "She isn't getting better."

Beatrice gazed at her friend silently for a moment, taking in the weight of Evelyn's words. She knew how much Venus meant to Evelyn—the dog was more than just a pet; she was a confidante and faithful companion who had seen Evelyn through both joyous and challenging times.

"Oh, my dear," Beatrice finally whispered, her vibrant eyes softening with empathy. She reached out to place a comforting hand on Evelyn's shoulder, the touch steadying like the root of an age-old oak tree. "Tell me everything."

And so, Evelyn did. She spoke of the once lively Venus, now lying lethargic in her bed, refusing food and water. Of the nights spent sitting by Venus's side, trying to comfort her with gentle words and tender strokes. She recounted how Venus's once bright eyes had dimmed, how her soft whimpers echoed in the hushed silence of their home.

Beatrice listened attentively as Evelyn spilled out her worries. Her azure gaze remained steady and understanding, absorbing the pain that seeped from Evelyn's every word. Around them, the market buzzed with the sound of vendors shouting, but the children were not laughing. Immersed in social media, parents ignored their offspring, who wandered aimlessly, their joy absent from the usual rhythm of life. The heartache unfolding between Beatrice and Evelyn went unnoticed in the distracted, digital haze surrounding them.

Once Evelyn finished talking, Beatrice squeezed her friend's shoulder, lending a silent vow of support. She looked deep into Evelyn's tired eyes, searching for words that might offer solace. But she knew that no mere words could douse the pain of seeing someone you love suffer.

"Evelyn," Beatrice began, her voice carrying the heaviness of the situation. "I have trodden enough paths and met enough souls to know this—sometimes, the strength of love and will can be stronger than any ailment."

Beatrice reached into a pocket hidden within her vibrant skirts, pulling out a small leather pouch adorned with symbols similar to those on her amulet. She carefully handed it to Evelyn.

"This is a charm, a protective necklace that a wise old woman gave me during my passage through the deserts of Sahrae," she explained, her voice barely above a whisper. "She told me it carries the energy of life itself, harnessed from the essence of the desert sun."

Evelyn looked at the pouch, her eyes awash with a mixture of hope and apprehension. As she gently held it, there was a warmth that seemed to seep into her skin, as if the charm was alive with an energy of its own. She could feel the fine grains of sand embedded in the leather, each one carrying the tales of faraway lands and ancient wisdom.

"I... I don't know what to say, Beatrice," Evelyn muttered, her voice heavy with emotion. She glanced up at her friend, her eyes searching for answers in a sea of uncertainty.

Beatrice simply smiled, her eyes dancing with empathy and reassurance. "You don't have to say anything, dear," she softly answered. "Just believe. And place it around Venus's neck tonight."

Evelyn nodded slowly, cradling the charm close to her heart. She felt a strange sense of serenity washing over her—a calming wave that quelled the raging storm within.

As Beatrice watched Evelyn's features soften in the tender glow of hope, she knew it was time to reveal a truth long kept hidden. With her heart pounding in her chest, she hesitated for a moment before drawing a deep breath. The world seemed to still around them, the noise of the market fading into a distant hum.

"Evelyn," Beatrice began, her voice steady yet laced with an unspoken tension. "This charm contains more than just the energy of life... it holds magic." The last word hung in the air like a delicate note played on a harp, both ethereal and powerful.

Evelyn looked up sharply, surprise overtaking the calm that had momentarily washed over her features. She stared at Beatrice, her eyes widening as the realization of what was just revealed seeped into her consciousness.

"Magic?" Evelyn echoed, her hand instinctively clenching around the charm. She looked from Beatrice to the pouch in her hand and back again, disbelief etched across her face.

"Yes, magic," Beatrice affirmed, her gaze steady. "Not the kind spun in fairy tales or whispered about in hushed tones at the tavern, but a subtle and potent energy. The kind that could only be borne from the heart of the world itself."

She reached out then, touching the charm still cradled in Evelyn's hand with a gentle reverence. Her fingertips grazed the worn leather pouch, her touch so feather-light that it was almost imperceptible. As she made contact with the charm, a soft glow emanated from it, bathing their hands in a warm golden light that seemed to pulse with life.

"This is not some simple trinket, Evelyn," she said, her voice dropping to a whisper as she locked eyes with her friend. "This is an echo of Sahrae itself—of its burning suns and endless sands. It is imbued with the wisdom and strength of those who have trodden those dunes for generations upon generations. It is a reservoir of the power that pervades everything, from the grandest mountain to the tiniest grain of sand."

Beatrice paused, letting the words sink into Evelyn's consciousness. She pulled her hand back, letting the glowing charm settle once more in Evelyn's palm. A hush had fallen over them. Even the chaotic bustle of the market seemed distant and subdued—a world away from this solemn moment.

"I do not give this to you lightly," Beatrice continued, her gaze never wavering from Evelyn's wide-eyed stare. "This magic... it could be dangerous if wielded without understanding or respect. But I trust you, Evelyn."

Her words were firm and resolute, echoing with an unspoken promise. The air around them seemed to shimmer with energy, as if acknowledging the gravity of what was being given and received.

Evelyn was silent for a long while, her eyes fixed on the glowing charm in her hand. The warm pulsating light felt oddly comforting, like the gentle touch of a mother soothing a child's fears away. Her mind was a whirlwind of confusion and disbelief, yet there was an underlying sense of understanding—a deep, resonant truth that rang clearer than any doubts.

"Beatrice," Evelyn finally whispered, her voice crackling with awe and apprehension. "I don't... I don't understand how this is possible. But... but I do feel it." She frowned slightly, her hand clenching tighter around the charm. The glow intensified for a moment before settling down to a soft, steady pulse.

"That's good," Beatrice said gently, her eyes twinkling with approval and something else—perhaps pride? "Feeling it is the first step towards understanding, Evelyn."

"And... and what do I do now?" Evelyn asked, her voice wavering slightly as she faced the enormity of what she held in her hands.

Beatrice paused, considering Evelyn's question. After a moment she answered, "Now, Evelyn, you learn to embrace it. To walk with it, as you would a dear friend. It is not just about casting spells or bending elements to your will. This is about understanding the heartbeat of Sahrae itself and becoming one with it." She gestured around them, to the bustling marketplace, the sky overhead.

"Every whisper of the wind, every grain shifting beneath our feet, every heart beating in this marketplace—they are all part of Sahrae's music," she continued. "They are all fragments of its magic. To wield magic is to understand this symphony, this beautiful dance of creation and dissolution. It is to become a co-creator in this wondrous ballet."

Beatrice stood for a moment, her robe billowing around her with graceful drama.

"However, Evelyn," she added with a sobering tone, "you also need to ensure you handle this with caution. The element of surprise is powerful, but the wisdom to wield such magic safely and responsibly is paramount." Beatrice reached into her robe and pulled out a roll of parchment, bound by a taut crimson thread.

She unfurled it carefully, revealing a list of items penned in her fluid script. The names were exotic, each one resonating with an aura of ancient wisdom. "This," she said, lightly running a finger down the parchment, "is the Codicil of Confluence."

Beatrice handed the list to Evelyn, who accepted it with wide-eyed curiosity. Her eyes danced over the parchment as she read aloud: "Shard of Sabra Moonstone... Lumen Ivy... Flameheart Elixir... Sliver of Eonwood... Seven Stranded Knot of Whisper Wind Thread... Aeon Tear."

"Collect these," Beatrice instructed, her smile etched with a softness, "For they are not mere items of the earth. They are bearers of elemental power, remnants of forgotten realms and secret keepers of Sahrae's wisdom. Each holds a piece of the cosmic puzzle, a unique key to unlocking the magic within you."

She paused, allowing Evelyn a moment to absorb the weight of her words. The bustling marketplace seemed to fade away as Evelyn focused solely on the parchment in her hands and its unearthly symbols.

"Once you have collected them all," Beatrice continued thoughtfully, "We will perform a ritual. It is through this process that you will channel your inherent magic and unleash your true potential."

Evelyn nodded slowly, a sense of determination settling upon her features. Her heart pounded with anticipation, fear, and excitement all rolled into one complex ball of emotions. She held the Codicil of Confluence up to the light, watching as the gold-inked script shimmered enchantingly.

"I will be at your house tonight, at the stroke of seven," Beatrice said, pulling Evelyn from her trance. "Make sure you have all the items ready. We must not delay any longer."

Evelyn's gaze met Beatrice's, her eyes wide with promise and worry. "And if I can't find all the items...?"

"The market traders will have most of what you need," Beatrice reassured her, her voice firm yet kind. "And for those that are more elusive, remember this, Evelyn: the universe conspires in our favor when our intentions are pure. You will find them."

Evelyn nodded solemnly, squeezing the parchment tighter in her grip. She felt a strange mixture of fear and readiness coursing through her veins. This was it. This was the beginning of something she could barely comprehend.

Beatrice turned and walked into the crowd, her robes rustling as she moved towards the exit. She paused at the threshold, her back to Evelyn, and with a voice just loud enough to reach the young woman, she said, "I knew you needed Beatrice today." The words lingered in the air, imbued with an undercurrent of promise and impending change. Her form then disappeared into the bustle of the marketplace, leaving behind a charged silence.

Evelyn stood there for a moment longer, clutching the Codicil of Confluence tightly in her hands. The weight of the parchment seemed to ground her amidst the whirlwind of thoughts. She felt a profound connection to something ancient and all-encompassing, something that flowed through her veins like an unspoken melody.

There was magic waiting to be awakened, power pulsating beneath the surface of reality. And now she held the key—a list with names as cryptic as they were bewitching, the guide to her destiny woven intricately in arcane symbols that danced in golden ink. Beatrice had shared with her a secret piece of Sahrae's wisdom. She had a chance to unlock her true potential, and she wasn't going to let it slip away.

With a newfound determination in her eyes, Evelyn started walking quickly towards the first stall that caught her eye, filled with an array of glittering crystals and dusky gemstones. She held the Codicil tightly as she scanned the array for a shard of Sabra Moonstone—her first step towards destiny.

The marketplace was bustling with life, the air filled with the enticing smell of exotic spices and the chatter of eager merchants. Evelyn wandered from stall to stall, her search becoming a quest through a labyrinth of mounted gems, rare herbs, and exquisite feathers.

She found the Sabra Moonstone among the radiant crystals in a jeweler's booth. It shimmered against its more mundane counterparts, reflecting hues of deepest midnight blue flecked with tiny points of silvery light—like stars held captive in stone. Evelyn felt an immediate connection to it, a magnetic pull that seemed to echo deep within her own spirit. She exchanged a handful of coins with the merchant, who smiled at her knowingly as if he too could sense the importance of her quest.

Next on her list was the Lumen Ivy, a plant known to grow in the deepest shadows yet show the brightest colors. With each step, Evelyn felt drawn further into this world of concealed power and lost magic—a world she was only now beginning to comprehend.

She found the plant in the stall of a peculiar horticulturist who had a garden of exotic flora arrayed before him. The Lumen Ivy grew in an ornate pot, its leaves radiating an iridescent glow that betrayed its mundane appearance. At her approach, it seemed to respond, shifting colors from an electric blue to a luminescent white. Evelyn exchanged another handful of coins for the potted plant and tucked it into her bag.

As dusk approached and the marketplace began to wind down, Evelyn had gathered most of the items on the list—

the Flameheart Elixir from a wandering alchemist, a sliver of Eonwood from a grizzled woodsman, and a seven-stranded knot of Whisper Wind thread from a blind old weaver who smiled warmly as she handed the silken strands over.

Only one item remained, something called the 'Aeon Tear,' and Evelyn was at a loss. It was listed last on the Codicil and no explanation was given as to what it might be or where she might find it. The sun had set and the marketplace was clearing out, stalls were closing, and torches being lit. Under the growing cloak of night, her hopes of finding this last item dwindled.

Feeling somewhat defeated, Evelyn decided to rest at a nearby well. As she sat down on its cold stone edge, her attention was caught by persistent twinkling in the water below. A reflection of the stars above perhaps? But when she peered closer into the well's inky depths, she noticed something amiss.

The reflection didn't match the constellation overhead. Curiosity piqued, she reached in, her fingers breaking through the mirror-like surface of the well. To her astonishment, she found an object nestled within. With a pull of effort, she brought it up to examine under the flickering torchlight. The object was a tear-shaped gem, almost fluid in its luminescent beauty. It shimmered with each shift of light, radiating myriad colors before settling into a calm, cool azure—like the color of the starry night sky itself. An Aeon Tear.

Evelyn's heart pounded in her chest as she held it aloft. It was more beautiful than anything she had ever seen, and the energy it radiated was striking. This was what she had been searching for—the final piece of her journey, hidden not amongst the stalls and shouting merchants but in an unassuming well where no one thought to look.

Overwhelmed with joy and relief, she clutched the Aeon Tear to her chest. The delicate gem pulsed softly against her, in rhythm with her own heartbeat. She felt an influx of energy surge through her veins, a subtle warmth spreading from the pit of her stomach to the tips of her fingers. As she clutched the Aeon Tear, it seemed the very air around her shimmered, a tangible wave of magic emanating from the gem and seeping into her. It was different, powerful—terrifyingly so—and yet, at the same time, completely right.

The whispers of power it emitted echoed within her veins, resonating with the magnetism she had felt when acquiring the first item, the Starstone. It was as if everything was falling into place, each magical item she had collected leading her precisely to this moment.

The marketplace had been deserted by now; its vibrant colors muted in the soft glow of torchlight that crawled upon its stone-laid paths. The merchant stalls stood vacant and silent, their wares hidden away for the night. She stood alone with the Aeon Tear clutched in her hand and a swell of anticipation blooming within her chest.

With profound reverence, she placed the Aeon Tear in a velvet pouch along with the other items. She felt a magnetic pull and heard a soft humming as the objects made contact, harmonizing with a rhythm that felt almost alive.

She left the marketplace, its cobbled streets echoing her steps and the murmur of the night breeze. The torches cast long, dancing shadows that frolicked across her path as she wound her way through serpentine alleys towards her home—a tranquil cottage nestled in the heart of a whispering wood.

Her little abode was shrouded in an uncanny silence that made her heart flutter. It was as though her dwelling held its breath in quiet anticipation, yearning for the grand event to unfold. The moon bathed the cottage in silver light, casting exquisite shadows on the roughly hewn timbers and illuminating the overstuffed herbs hanging from her eaves.

Evelyn unlocked the door, stepping into her cozy living room where a soft fire glowed in the hearth, the crackling of burning wood the only sound to break the silence. The warm and inviting scent of dried sage and lavender filled the room, emanating from the small bundles she had hung by the hearth to dry.

Her eyes fell upon Venus, her faithful canine companion. The old dog lay curled on her favorite woollen rug near the hearth, her breathing ragged, her remaining eye dimmed with fatigue.

Evelyn felt a pang of sorrow at the sight of her companion. Venus had been with her from the beginning, her constant confidante and faithful friend. The dog's once lustrous coat was now peppered with gray, her boundless energy replaced with weary slumber. She was old, too old, and time had taken its toll relentlessly. But tonight, Evelyn hoped to change all that.

"Venus," she murmured, her voice soft as the flutter of a moth's wings in the quiet room. "Hold on, my dear. We will save you tonight."

The dog lifted her head at the sound of her name, gazing up at Evelyn with a trust that was as unwavering as it was heartbreaking. Her eyes held a depth of understanding that spoke of years together—of secrets shared, adventures braved, and the unspoken bond between two souls.

Evelyn sank to her knees beside Venus. With gentle hands, she stroked the dog's coat, feeling the coarse texture of her age under her fingertips. Her eyes wandered to the velvet pouch secured at her waist. She had a plan, a hope born from ancient lore and whispered tales of powerful magic. The items she carried—the Starstone, the Aeon Tear—were said to possess healing properties, and tonight she would test their mystical might.

A resounding knock echoed through the silence of her home, pulling Evelyn from her thoughts. Startled, she glanced up at the old grandfather clock that stood like a sentinel in the corner of her living room—it was exactly 7 pm. The rhythmic ticking seemed to echo louder with each passing second as the beats of her heart quickened in anticipation.

Taking a deep breath, she rose from Venus's side and moved towards the door. The hearty oak seemed larger than life under her trembling hand as she reached for the brass knob, its coolness grounding her. With an intake of breath and a whispering prayer to whichever gods still watched over lost mortals, she turned the knob and opened the door.

Chapter 2 -'The Spell'

As Evelyn opened the door, she was greeted by the sight of Beatrice standing in the glow of the moon. The pale light seemed to give her an aura of power and worldly knowledge, casting shadows on her features that only added to her mysterious allure. Her stance exuded confidence, and her piercing gaze held a hint of danger, making Evelyn's heart skip a beat. She was like a goddess bathed in moonlight, enchanting and untouchable at the same time.

"Step inside, Beatrice," she beckoned. Beatrice stepped over the threshold with cautious curiosity, her gaze drinking in every detail. She disrobed her woollen coat with precision, revealing an ensemble of pale silk and intricate lace beneath. She was careful to fold it over her arm before venturing deeper into the room.

"Did you manage to find everything on the list?" Beatrice queried, her gaze never straying from the expanse of the room.

Evelyn nodded, a rush of giddiness coursing through her veins. She beckoned Beatrice inside, into the comfortable chaos of her home. A soft glow enveloped the room, shadows dancing on the walls from the flickering flames in the hearth. Clearing off two seats piled high with books, Evelyn revealed a small table laden with an array of peculiar items.

Beatrice surveyed everything with wide, appreciative eyes, her heart pounding like a drum against her chest. "Yes, Beatrice," Evelyn murmured, her voice barely more than a whisper. "Every item." She moved to the table, her hand hovering over each object before finally resting on a small velvet box. "Including this." She opened it slowly, revealing the Aeon Tear tucked inside—a gem of unimaginable beauty.

Beatrice exhaled sharply, her eyes widening in shock as she gazed upon the Aeon Tear. It glowed softly in the dim light, casting an otherworldly radiance around the room. Its surface was smooth and polished, seemingly liquid under the warm glow of the lamp. The stone was an unworldly mix of colours, swirling hues of blues and greens, like looking into the heart of a star.

"You found it…" Beatrice breathed out, her words hardly above a whisper as she reached out tentatively towards it. Her fingertips barely grazed its surface, yet she pulled back sharply as though the cold touch had burned her. "The Aeon Tear… It truly exists." Her voice was filled with awe that echoed through the room.

Evelyn's voice caught in her throat as she spoke, thick with emotion. "Pardon," she said, her eyes searching Beatrice's face for an explanation. "Beatrice, I don't understand. You gave me the list and now you act surprised that I have found it. Why?" Her hands trembled slightly as she waited for a response, the tension between them lay heavy in the air.

Beatrice fell into a pensive silence before her eyes flicked to Evelyn, gratitude softening the lines of her face. "My dear Evelyn, there are forces at play that I cannot fully comprehend or reveal at this moment. But we must act swiftly if we want to save Venus," she spoke in hushed tones. "What I can tell you is this Aeon Tear… it holds the power of a spell that was thought to have been lost in time."

Evelyn blinked, her lips parting in surprise. "A lost spell?" she echoed, a sense of awe creeping into her voice. She glanced back at the Aeon Tear, the gem seeming to glow brighter under her scrutiny.

Beatrice's eyes widened with a mix of awe and fear as she edged closer to the table, drawn in by the pulsating glow of the beautiful gem. "Yes," she confirmed, her voice trembling with reverence. "It is an ancient spell of empowerment and rebirth... a spell that can only be unlocked by one pure of heart and appears when a prophesied fate must be fulfilled." Her hand shook as it hovered over the gem, feeling its otherworldly power beckoning her towards destiny.

The atmosphere in the room deepened into a profound silence as Evelyn absorbed this new information. Her mind raced with questions and unspoken fears, yet none of them found their way out of her mouth.

Beatrice broke the silence once again, her voice whisper-soft yet powerful at the same time. "We must prepare," she announced decisively, addressing Evelyn without looking away from the radiant stone. "Bring me hot water and get a pestle and mortar ready."

Without wasting any time, Evelyn moved toward the stove, placing a pot of water upon it. The fire danced beneath, casting flickering shadows on the walls that seemed to mimic their growing anxiety. As the water slowly began to heat, Evelyn reached for a pestle and mortar that had been pushed to the far end of the table. It was a relic, passed down through generations, its stone surface worn smooth by countless uses.

Her eyes flicked towards Beatrice, who now stood by the window, a silhouette against the luminescent moonlight streaming into the room. She watched as Beatrice unlatched the window, pushing it open. The whisper of the night breeze seeped into the room, making the flame beneath the pot waver and dance even more wildly.

"Evelyn," Beatrice called over her shoulder, her voice cutting through the hum of boiling water and rustling of leaves outside. "We need the moonlight."

Evelyn nodded in understanding. Moving swiftly yet carefully, she cleared a space on the table closest to the window and moved the Aeon Tear to its center. As the moonlight hit it, the stone pulsed with an unearthly light, casting prismatic colors around the room.

"Hand me the charm I gave you for Venus, Evelyn," Beatrice extended her palm, the moonlight making her old, scarred hand seem mystical.

Evelyn reached for the leather pouch that held the charm. As she revealed the charm from the pouch under the moonlight and the glow of the Aeon Tear, it was now on a gold necklace, the perfect size to fit Venus's neck. The charm was a dull gold but beautiful necklace, with a pendant that looked like two gold diamonds, intricately created and set on wings. Evelyn did not remember it being so beautiful and intricately made.

Evelyn's hand reached instinctively for the leather pouch that held the charm given to her by Beatrice earlier that day in the bustling market. With trembling hands, Evelyn pulled out the Aeon Tear from the protective pouch. Its blinding light engulfed her, blurring her vision and sending a jolt of electricity through her body. The charm glimmered even brighter, its intensity almost too much to bear as it pulsated with otherworldly energy. Evelyn could feel a deep sense of power emanating from the object, but she could not look away as its light reflected off her face, casting an eerie glow in the room.

In her palm now lay a beautiful gold necklace, and it felt as if a fire had been ignited within the charm. The weight of it was more substantial, and every fleck of gold on its surface seemed to come alive, creating intricate shadows that danced across Evelyn's skin. The entire necklace was made of gold.

The pendant was a masterpiece of intricate design, two sharp triangles adorned with fierce feathers that seemed to pulse with energy. The golden wings that held them aloft radiated power and grace, as if they could take flight at any moment. It was a symbol of strength and determination, a talisman that beckoned for greatness to be achieved.

Evelyn gawked at the charm, her mind whirling with thoughts. "Beatrice," she breathed in awe, "it's beautiful. How is this possible?" Her breath hitched as she delicately traced the pulsating wings of the pendant.

"No need for fear, dear Evelyn," Beatrice reassured, her voice calm yet filled with a quiet intensity. She stepped away from the window, her figure bathed in silver moonlight. With an air of sacredness, she moved towards Evelyn and extended her scarred hand to receive the charm.

Evelyn handed it over, the warmth of the charm lingering on her skin. Beatrice held it under the luminous rays of moonlight, and together they watched as it seemed to hum with a life of its own. The charm's glow became more radiant in Beatrice's possession, as if recognizing its rightful owner.

"Watch carefully," Beatrice instructed, holding the charm above the Aeon Tear which rested on the table. As the charm was hovered over the Tear, it seemed to respond energetically. The charm began to oscillate, and its frequential hum grew steadily louder. Even without touching, it interacted with the Tear, their lights dancing in a ballet of celestial vibrancy.

Beatrice closed her eyes and began to chant softly under her breath. Words from an ancient language filled the room, enveloping Evelyn in a sense of tranquility and wonder; she felt an incredible surge of energy flow through her. The room buzzed as if charged with anticipation while shadows flickered and danced in the radiating light.

Beatrice's chant grew louder, her voice filled with power:

"In lumine lunae, vires antiqua voco,

Aureum vinculum, anima et corpus coniunge,

Perpetua lux, sanitatem redde."

Beatrice repeated the chant in her native tongue out loud:

"In the light of the moon, I call upon ancient powers,

Tear of Aeon, Golden bond, unite soul and body,

Eternal light, restore health."

With every word that Beatrice chanted, the charm throbbed more intensely. Suddenly, with a swift motion that left Evelyn gasping, Beatrice threw the charm toward Venus. The necklace arced through the air, a shower of light trailing behind it as it flew with determination across the room. There was a muted gasp from Evelyn as the charm clasped itself around Venus's neck with uncanny precision. The dog growled in response, yet not in fear but in a certain kind of understanding, as if her pain was being eased by the charm's presence.

Beatrice turned to face Evelyn, her eyes gleaming with satisfaction. "The necklace is now where it belongs," she declared assertively, her gaze unwavering. "And now we can proceed." The words echoed through the room, each syllable emphasizing the sense of gravity and importance of what was happening.

Venus lifted her head, her remaining eye glinting with an otherworldly brilliance as she regained some strength and moved with newfound energy. However, it was short-lived, and her head soon sank back down to the ground.

"The charm's power is immense, but her strength is faltering. We have to act quickly," Beatrice said. Her voice was calm, her tone level, but the worry etched on her face spoke volumes. She moved to Venus's side, kneeling gently on the woven woolen carpet that adorned the floor of the room. Her hands hovered above the charm, and with a deep breath, she began to chant again.

This time Evelyn could see the air shimmer around Beatrice's hands as she chanted in an ancient language known only to a few. She could feel it too—a prickly sensation that defied explanation. The air thickened and grew warm, filled with latent energy ready to burst forth at any given second.

Beatrice's voice rose and fell, creating a rhythmic symphony against the backdrop of silence that filled the rest of the room. Words turned into ropey strands of light that flowed from Beatrice's lips and onto Venus, wrapping around her body.

Beatrice's piercing gaze locked onto Evelyn as she spoke with a sense of urgency, her voice nearly trembling. "Evelyn," she hissed, "grind the items you collected today. It is imperative that they are added in the exact order listed. And remember, this must be done under the moonlight—it is the only time when the stars align and our bond with Venus is strong enough to save her." Beatrice's words hung heavy in the air, filled with urgency and a hint of desperation. "Do not fail us now, for love is our only hope."

Without wasting any further time, Evelyn jumped into action. She frantically started gathering the items she had collected earlier that day—the Shard of Sabra Moonstone, the Lumen Ivy, and the Flameheart Elixir. The list was exhaustive, but she knew each item was to be ground in its own sequence under the moonlight to allow for the cosmic energy to infuse it. She continued, collecting the Sliver of Eonwood, the Seven Stranded Knot of Whisper Wind Thread, and finally, the Aeon Tear. Each item shimmered with its own unique energy, ready to play its part in the powerful ritual.

As she began, the first item—the Shard of Sabra Moonstone—was turned to dust under the ancient brass pestle and mortar. As it disintegrated, a strange smell filled the room, a curious mix of fresh grass after rain and something tangibly unearthly. There was something soothing about it, as though it carried with it the freshness and life from another world.

Around her, sparks began to fly from the grinding process as the particles collided against one another. They shimmered around her in a mesmerizing light show, each tiny point of light imbued with a spectrum of colors that danced and flickered evocatively. The faint whisper of the grindstone filled the room, a melodious symphony harmonizing with Beatrice's continuous chanting.

As she moved on to the next item, a sense of profound anticipation permeated the air. Her hands, steady with a determined resolve, continued their task. The Lumen Ivy crumbled beneath her touch, adding another layer to the ominously beautiful aroma wafting in the room. The scent was intoxicating, a blend of crisp autumn leaves and the sweet tartness of ripe berries, with an undertone that hinted at the mysteries of nature.

An eerie glow bathed Evelyn in its otherworldly luminescence as the particles started to intertwine with each other, forming an intricate lattice of cosmic energy around her. It was as if they were dancing to an ancient rhythm only they could hear, their movements wild yet synchronized, chaotic yet purposeful.

A raw energy buzzed through her nerves as she continued grinding, the next item—the Flameheart Elixir—adding a third dimension to the fragrance that filled the room. The scent of the elixir was heady, as if it had captured the essence of a summer storm, conjuring images of the heavens opening up and pouring down its might while sunlight peeked through the menacing clouds.

The grinding process was demanding and challenging, yet there was a sense of serene calm that enveloped Evelyn. It was as if the moon's rays were bestowing upon her an insurmountable strength—one that would allow her to endure until Venus was saved.

As she handled the last item on the list to be ground together—the Seven Stranded Knot of Whisper Wind Thread—her heart pounded in sync with Beatrice's rhythmic chants. As she ground it to dust, it released a fragrance so divine that it transcended all those preceding it. It was reminiscent of a forgotten time, carrying an aroma that seemed to contain within it the mysteries of ancient civilizations and lost worlds.

As the final particles of the Seven Stranded Knot of Whisper Wind Thread were absorbed by the bustling air, Evelyn finished her part of the ritual. With a breath heavy with anticipation, she gently tipped the brass mortar, allowing the resulting concoction to fall into the pot stationed over the fire.

"Excellent," Beatrice croaked out, her voice raspy from the continuous chanting. Her eyes, though fatigued, shimmered with relentless determination. "Add them to the pot on the fire," she rasped, barely audible over the crackling flames. "And as you do, recite the words on the back of the parchment. Let the light of the Aeon Tear guide you."

Evelyn flipped over the parchment and gasped when she saw that the ancient spell was now written in shimmering gold ink. How had it appeared there? She didn't have time to think about it as she leaned over the cauldron and began to chant.

"Spirits of old, hear my plea,

From ancient bonds, I call to thee.

With moon's glow and phoenix fire,

Heal this soul, fulfill desire."

But then something took control of Evelyn. Her eyes shone with an otherworldly light as she continued to speak in an ancient tongue without thought or control:

"Venite, spiritus antiqui, adjuvate nos.

Lumen lunae, ignis phoenicis,

Sanate hanc animam, complite votum.

In lumine et amore, restitute vitam,

Ut floreat iterum, sicut priscis temporibus."

As she spoke, the room filled with a blinding light. The air crackled with power and a warm wind swirled around her, carrying petals and feathers into the air. The light grew brighter, enveloping Evelyn in its radiance. She could sense the presence of the ancient spirits, their energy merging with her own.

For a moment, everything stood still. And then with a soft sigh, Venus stirred. Her eye fluttered open and for the first time in days, it was clear and alert. Evelyn's heart soared as she watched her beloved pet look back at her.

"Venus?" she whispered, tears streaming down her face. "Are you okay?"

Though Venus couldn't speak, Evelyn could feel the overwhelming emotions of love and gratitude emanating from her. She didn't know if it was the spell or the ancient spirits that had answered her call.

Evelyn carefully lifted Venus and placed her on her lap, cradling her gently. She could feel the faint warmth of renewed life coursing through her small body. The cottage, once filled with tension and worry, now seemed to breathe a sigh of relief alongside Evelyn. As she stroked Venus's fur, she whispered, "We'll take it one day at a time, my sweet girl. You're a fighter, and we'll get through this together."

Outside, the enchanted woods seemed to respond to the successful spell. The leaves rustled with a newfound vigor, and a soft, surreal glow illuminated the trees, as if the ancient spirits were expressing their approval.

Venus soon drifted into a peaceful sleep by the fire, her breathing more steady and her little body more at ease. Evelyn gently covered her with a warm blanket, ensuring she was comfortable. As she did, Beatrice, who had assisted with the ritual, stepped forward.

"The spell is done," Beatrice said softly. "Now, only time will tell."

Evelyn nodded, her exhaustion clearly visible. Beatrice continued, "I must go now. Both of you will sleep well tonight."

"I'll be in touch in the morning to see how Venus is doing," Beatrice added, giving Evelyn a reassuring smile before heading towards the door.

"Thank you, Beatrice," Evelyn said, her gratitude evident. She watched as Beatrice left, feeling a deep sense of appreciation for her friend's support.

Moments after Beatrice departed, a chilling howl echoed through the night, sending a shiver down Evelyn's spine. She quickly moved to the window and closed it, bolting it securely. The howl of a wolf was unusual so close to her cottage, and the sound filled her with an uneasy fear.

Evelyn returned to Venus's side, kneeling down to kiss her goodnight. "I love you, Venus," she whispered, her voice filled with tenderness. She carefully reached into her pocket and, to her surprise, found a small black eye patch. She didn't remember placing it there, but it seemed like a fitting symbol of Venus's resilience.

With gentle hands, she carefully placed the eye patch over Venus's left eye, ensuring it was comfortable and secure. "There," she murmured softly, "now you look like the brave little warrior you are."

Satisfied that Venus was resting peacefully, Evelyn finally allowed herself to go to bed. She felt a deep exhaustion settle over her, the events of the day weighing heavily on her mind and body. As she lay down, she couldn't help but think of the journey that still lay ahead, but for now, she took comfort in the progress they had made.

As she drifted off to sleep, Evelyn felt a renewed sense of hope. She hoped the ancient spirits had heard her plea. For tonight, they would both rest, their bond stronger than ever and their spirits intertwined with the magic that now flowed through their lives.

Chapter 3 – 'The Enemy Revealed'

The next morning, Beatrice sipped her lemon iced tea, savoring the refreshing tang as she basked in the sun. Her garden, a sanctuary of tranquility, was in full bloom. Roses of every color imaginable filled the air with their intoxicating fragrance. Climbing roses draped elegantly over trellises, while delicate blooms peeked from beneath lush green foliage. A cobblestone path meandered through the garden, leading to a small, wrought-iron table where Beatrice sat, enjoying her solitary breakfast.

Dressed in a vibrant patchwork skirt that swayed with every breeze and a blouse adorned with embroidered sunflowers, Beatrice's eclectic style matched her quirky personality. Her silver hair was pinned up with an assortment of colorful clips, and she wore mismatched earrings—one a dangling crescent moon, the other a sparkling star.

As she set her cup down, the sound of small, quick footsteps drew her attention. A mischievous monkey named Chico scampered into the garden, his eyes twinkling with curiosity. Chico, one of Beatrice's trusted companions, climbed up the back of a nearby chair and settled there, watching her intently. This was no ordinary monkey; Chico was a vigilant observer of the natural world, always ready to assist Beatrice with his keen senses and playful nature.

"Good morning, Chico," Beatrice greeted, her voice filled with affection.

Chico chattered softly, his expressive eyes communicating his message. He hopped from the chair to the table, picking up a small twig and drawing a circle around a pebble. Beatrice watched intently, understanding his gestures.

"The spell has worked," Beatrice interpreted from his actions, her heart lifting momentarily. Chico then mimed a dramatic fall, clutching his chest and pointing towards the direction of Evelyn's cottage.

"What do you mean, Chico? Is something wrong?" Beatrice asked, her concern growing.

Chico's eyes widened with urgency. He mimed dark, creeping figures with his hands and pointed frantically towards Evelyn's cottage again. He then pretended to be surrounded, looking fearful and defensive.

Beatrice's heart skipped a beat as she realized what he was conveying. "Evelyn's cottage is surrounded by beasts. Dark creatures are closing in. You must hurry."

Chico nodded vigorously, his eyes pleading for her to understand the gravity of the situation. Beatrice stood up, her resolve hardening. "Thank you, Chico. We must go now."

Shock and concern washed over Beatrice. She stood abruptly, her chair scraping against the cobblestones. "Beasts? How did this happen?"

Chico indicated urgently with a flurry of gestures and frantic movements that there was no time to explain. He pointed towards the woods and then mimed running with exaggerated urgency.

Beatrice nodded, her eccentric attire fluttering as she moved swiftly. She grabbed a knitted shawl in vibrant hues of purple and green, draping it over her shoulders. With a determined stride, she headed towards the garden gate, her numerous bracelets clinking musically with each step.

Chico scampered ahead, his agile movements a blur as he darted from branch to branch, acting as a sentinel in the trees. Beatrice's heart pounded with a mix of fear and urgency. The path through the garden seemed longer than usual, each step heavy with the weight of the unknown danger threatening Evelyn and Venus.

Beatrice pushed through the garden gate, her mind racing. She had to reach Evelyn's cottage before it was too late. The usually serene walk through the woods was now filled with an undercurrent of tension, every rustle of leaves and snap of a twig amplifying her anxiety.

As she hurried along the forest path, the canopy of trees above cast shifting shadows on the ground, creating an eerie play of light and dark. Chico moved just ahead, his presence a constant reassurance with his quick, deliberate motions.

"Stay close, Chico," Beatrice called out, her voice breathless with exertion.

Chico glanced back, his keen eyes scanning the surroundings for any sign of danger, then nodded and continued leading the way.

Beatrice's mind raced with thoughts of the beasts Chico had indicated. What were they? How had they found Evelyn's cottage? She had to trust that the ancient magic within her could protect them all. She clutched the ruby necklace around her neck, a family heirloom infused with protective spells, drawing strength from its familiar weight.

As the sun rose over Evelyn's cottage, Evelyn awoke in a haze, her eyes struggling to focus after a restless night of sleep. She stumbled out of bed, still dressed in her rumpled pajamas, with her mind already consumed by thoughts of Venus. Her bare feet padded across the creaky floorboards as she made her way to the living room, expecting to find her faithful dog curled up by the warm fire. But instead, she was met with a shocking sight.

Lying on the rug in front of the fireplace was not Venus, but a naked woman with smooth, tanned skin and long straight black hair that fell just past her shoulders and a black eye patch. A sense of ancient mystery radiated from her very being. Evelyn's scream cut through the early morning silence as she took in this unexpected intruder.

The stranger jolted awake at the sound, just as startled as Evelyn. She scrambled to sit up, her eyes frantically searching their surroundings in confusion and fear. Around her neck hung the same gold necklace that had adorned Venus the previous night.

Evelyn's heart pounded as she backed away, keeping a cautious distance from the uninvited guest. "Who are you? What have you done with my dog?" she demanded.

The woman, still disoriented and clearly frightened, grabbed whatever objects were within reach—books from Evelyn's shelf—and hurled them towards her. As they crashed against the walls and furniture, she shouted in an ancient language that was foreign and unfamiliar to Evelyn: *"Anuara! Kalistraen! Malithra!"*

Evelyn dove behind a nearby table for cover as the two women faced off, each on opposite sides of the room. The mysterious woman's wild eyes were filled with a mix of fear and defiance, making it clear that she was not going down without a fight.

Outside the cottage, Beatrice's heart pounded in her chest as she reached the gate. Her breath caught in her throat as she saw the dark creatures surrounding the house. Wolves, with eyes glowing like burning coals, snarled and growled menacingly at her and Chico, who waved his fist at the wolves, and then hid behind Beatrice's leg.

Fear gripped Beatrice as she whispered to herself, "What have I done?" But she quickly gathered her courage and shouted, "Evelyn, I'm coming!"

Inside the cottage, the strange woman heard the commotion outside and sensed the danger. Fear turned to determination on her face as she turned to the window and shouted in an ancient tongue: *"Farnathra! Esthalar!"*

The wolves immediately backed off, creating a clear path to the front door. Beatrice was stunned by this display of power but didn't hesitate to hurry through the opened path, her heart racing.

As she burst through the front door, Beatrice's eyes widened in concern. "Evelyn, where are you?"

Evelyn peeked out from behind a table, her face pale with fear. "Beatrice, help!"

Taking in the scene—the naked woman, the thrown books, and the tense atmosphere—Beatrice's eyes fell upon the gold necklace around the woman's neck. Instantly recognizing it as the same one used during Venus' spell and a strange black eye patch, Beatrice realized with a start who the woman must be. "Venus?" she whispered, shock evident in her voice.

The woman, still wary but less aggressive now, slowly nodded in confirmation. Understanding dawned in her ancient eyes as she gazed at Beatrice. Taking a cautious step forward, Beatrice's voice was soft and soothing. "It's okay, we're here to help."

The tense standoff between them slowly dissolved into a fragile calm as they all realized the gravity of their situation.

The strange exotic woman was trembling slightly and spoke in her ancient tongue, her voice resonant and filled with a power that seemed to echo through time.

"Nimara se'ethra, calithran morreth," she intoned, her eyes wide with a mix of fear and defiance.

Chico scampered into the room, his small feet pattering sharply as he climbed onto the back of a chair, his eyes fixed on the woman. Outside, the wolves stood silently by the open front door, their growls subdued, their presence imposing but no longer threatening.

Beatrice, her heart still racing, looked around the room and noticed a stone on the table glowing with an otherworldly light. "The Aeon Tear Stone," she whispered, recognizing its power was growing.

Evelyn's eyes followed Beatrice's gaze, and she too saw the stone. As if guided by an unseen force, Beatrice reached out and touched the stone. The moment her fingers brushed against it, a warm light spread throughout the room, enveloping them all.

A strange sensation filled their minds, and suddenly, the ancient tongue of the woman became clear to them. "I am Selene," the woman said, her voice now understandable to Beatrice and Evelyn. "An ancient priestess, banished by powerful dark magic many centuries ago. The necklace is mine, a relic of my power."

Beatrice and Evelyn exchanged astonished glances but remained silent, listening intently.

Selene continued, her eyes shimmering with emotion. "The spell you cast to save Venus has broken the binding that held me. Venus and I are now entwined; I can transform between this form and hers. She was struck by dark magic, which sought to claim her life. But her pure soul was the key to freeing me, and in turn, I was able to save her."

Evelyn took a tentative step forward, her voice trembling. "So, Venus is still with us?"

Selene nodded. "Yes. Venus lives within me, and I within her. We share a bond now, stronger than any magic. She is happy, her spirit vibrant. She chose to help me, and I will protect her with all the power I have."

Beatrice, her mind racing, asked, "What must we do now?"

Selene's expression hardened with determination. "The dark magic that banished me is still at work. Those who wield it will seek to reclaim their hold. We must be prepared to fight. With the Aeon Tear Stone's power, we can communicate and work together to face the evil that threatens us all."

The room was charged with a sense of urgency and purpose. The glowing Aeon Tear Stone pulsed softly, a beacon of hope and strength. Evelyn nodded, her fear replaced with resolve. "We'll do whatever it takes to protect Venus, to protect us all."

Beatrice felt a surge of determination as well. "Together, we'll fight this darkness. We won't let it take over."

Selene's eyes shone with gratitude and fierce resolve. "Then let us prepare. The battle against the dark magic begins now, and we must be ready to face it together."

Selene noticed the glowing Aeon Tear Stone on the table and realized its potential. "We need to merge the Aeon Tear Stone with the necklace," she said, her voice steady. "It will strengthen our bond and power."

Selene nodded in agreement. She took a deep breath and began to chant, her voice echoing with ancient power:

"In lumine lunae et stellarum,

Nostra spiritus, ligare procul et prope.

Aeon Lacrima, cum magia clara,

Cor nostrum iunge et da nobis virtutem."

As she chanted, Selene held the Aeon Tear Stone above the necklace. The stone began to glow even brighter, its light merging with the necklace's aura. The room filled with a radiant light, casting long shadows and illuminating every corner.

The Aeon Tear Stone slowly descended, guided by an invisible force, until it touched the necklace. The two fused together seamlessly, the stone embedding itself into the center of the necklace, which now pulsed with an even greater power.

Selene smiled, her eyes reflecting the newfound strength. "It is done. Our bond is now stronger than ever."

Suddenly, there was a momentary pause, a void filled only by the soft humming of the Aeon Tear Stone, as Selene's gaze dropped to her own body—bare and unperturbed. A ripple of laughter escaped her lips, light and melodious, reverberating around the room like a beacon of joy amidst the tension. The stark contrast of the situation caught Evelyn and Beatrice off guard, pulling them from their solemn discussion into a world of mirthful absurdity.

Evelyn couldn't help but chuckle as well. "We're in this together, and we'll face whatever comes our way."

The light from the Aeon Tear Stone bathed them in its glow, solidifying the alliance between the ancient priestess, the modern-day witches, and the spirit of Venus. Their fates were now intertwined in the fight against the encroaching darkness.

"I should probably wear something more... suiting for our impending battle," Selene murmured with a playful smile tugging at her lips. She looked down, making an exaggerated show of taking stock of her nudity.

Evelyn blinked in surprise before releasing a laugh that echoed Selene's. "First, you need some clothes," she managed to say between giggles. "You can't go around with just a necklace on."

Selene clapped her hands together, her eyes twinkling with mischief. "Well, you see," she said, swirling the necklace hanging from her neck, "Venus tells me about a lovely white dress you have in your closet. She seems quite eager to wear it. Would that be acceptable?"

Evelyn sputtered into another round of laughter, clutching her sides. "Oh, Venus has indeed grown fond of that dress, hasn't she? You're welcome to it."

"Excellent!" Selene replied, beaming. She gracefully rose from her seat and turned towards Evelyn's closet with an eager bounce in her step. But then, she paused and glanced back over her shoulder at the two women, a slightly pensive look on her face.

"But perhaps," she started, tapping a finger against her lips thoughtfully, "I should cleanse myself first? Seeing as I've just emerged from... well, wherever I was."

Beatrice chuckled at this and nodded enthusiastically. "Yes!" she agreed heartily. "A shower would definitely seem appropriate, and might actually be quite refreshing."

Selene chuckled lightly, her laughter carrying the sweet sound of a silver bell. "Refreshing indeed," she agreed. "I feel as though I've been asleep for centuries!"

With that, she disappeared into Evelyn's bathroom, leaving the two witches chuckling and shaking their heads at the unexpected humor in a time of such immense danger and uncertainty.

Selene finally emerged from her shower, transformed. Pearls of water still clung to her skin like stardust; her hair shone radiantly in the light of the Aeon Tear Stone, now the centerpiece of the necklace.

The white dress clung to her slender form, flowing like moonlight into the room. The garment was of a different age, timeless in its elegance with its myriad layers of soft white silk falling to the floor. It was embroidered with delicate vines and flowers, each stitch a testament to Evelyn's craftsmanship. It seemed as though the material had been woven from the very essence of Venus herself; Selene shimmered with a soft glow, a goddess in her own right.

Evelyn and Beatrice watched in silent admiration as Selene spun briefly, her laughter carried on the air like a sacred melody. Her joy was infectious, filling the room with a lightness that belied their dire circumstances.

"And now," Selene declared, stepping into the center of the room, "it is time to take up arms against the dark forces encroaching upon this realm." Her voice took on a commanding tone, resonating with the power of the celestial bodies she represented. "Let's prepare for battle."

At these words, an eerie silence descended upon the room, the earlier levity replaced by a tangible sense of anticipation. Evelyn and Beatrice exchanged a glance before they both nodded in agreement. It was indeed time to face the darkness.

"But," Beatrice started, her voice tinged with both curiosity and apprehension, "what are we fighting exactly? And how can we make a difference? This magic is strong, but I fear our enemy is stronger."

Selene turned to gaze at them thoughtfully. "A valid question, Beatrice," she said in a soft voice that nonetheless echoed with authority. "We're not just fighting an enemy of flesh and blood; we're facing an entity that feeds off fear, despair, and chaos."

She paused for a moment, allowing the gravity of her words to sink in. "This entity," she continued, "is like a parasite that latches onto negativity and magnifies it. It's grown powerful over centuries of nurturing its strength through wars and strife. It's not a beast we can simply slay with sword or spell, it's an insidious force that thrives in the shadows of the human heart."

She touched the Aeon Tear Stone within her necklace, her fingers gently caressing its surface. The stone pulsed brighter in response, casting dancing shadows on the room's ancient tapestries. "That is why our task is twofold," she said gravely, her eyes reflecting the soft luminescence of the stone. "We must not only eliminate this entity but also heal the hearts it has infected."

Evelyn and Beatrice exchanged glances once more. This was a mission unlike any they had faced; a battle that demanded more than mere magic and might. But if Selene believed they could make a difference, then perhaps there was hope yet.

Selene took a deep breath, her eyes filled with a mix of sorrow and determination.

"The battle we face is not a simple one," she began, her voice steady and resolute. "The dark magic that banished me has evolved over the centuries. It is no longer just a force of nature but has intertwined itself with the advancements of humanity. It now controls computers, Artificial Intelligence known to you as AI, and other technologies, spreading its influence far and wide."

Beatrice and Evelyn listened intently, their faces pale but resolute. Selene continued, gesturing towards the wolves standing vigil by the door. "These wolves are not ordinary creatures. They are ancient protectors, tasked with tracking and confronting the evil force for centuries. They have seen it change and adapt, always seeking new ways to control and corrupt."

Evelyn glanced at the wolves, a newfound respect and understanding in her eyes. "How have they managed to follow the force for so long?" she asked.

Selene smiled softly. "They possess a bond with nature and the mystical energies of the world, much like we do. Their senses are heightened, and they can detect the subtle shifts in the balance of power. For centuries, they have fought to keep the darkness at bay, but now, the force has grown stronger, more insidious."

Beatrice nodded, her mind racing with the implications. "So, the dark magic uses technology to spread its influence?"

Selene nodded gravely. "Yes. It manipulates data, controls AI, and uses social media to sow discord and corruption among humans. It thrives on the chaos and negativity that these tools can generate. The wolves have seen how the force corrupts these technologies, turning them into weapons against us."

Selene took a deep breath, her eyes darkening as she prepared to reveal the depth of the danger they faced. "The evil force we contend with was once a man," she began, her voice low and grave. "A dark magician who, in his insatiable quest for power, sought to prolong his life indefinitely. Though he managed to extend his lifespan beyond that of any ordinary human, he could not conquer true immortality. His body began to fail him, and in his desperation, he devised a new plan."

Beatrice and Evelyn leaned in closer, captivated by Selene's words.

"He created a vast network," Selene continued, "a web of technology and magic intertwined. Within this network, he uploaded his essence—his mind, his will, and his greed. His name was Morghast, and his ambition knew no bounds. Morghast's essence now resides in this network, manipulating data, controlling artificial intelligence, and influencing the digital world. He feeds off the sadness, fear, and discord of humanity, becoming more powerful with every passing day."

The room seemed to darken as Selene spoke, the weight of her words heavy in the air.

"The wolves," she said, gesturing to the majestic creatures standing guard at the door, "have learned much about Morghast and his machinations. They have tracked his influence for centuries, watching as he evolved from a mere mortal into a pervasive digital entity. His network controls what people do, how they interact, and it sows seeds of despair and division among them."

Evelyn's eyes widened with understanding. "So, Morghast is behind the dark magic that attacked Venus?"

Selene nodded solemnly. "Yes. Morghast saw Venus's pure soul and your love for her as threats to his growing power. By attacking her, he aimed to weaken the light that opposes his darkness. But he did not anticipate the strength of your bond or the ancient magic you wielded to save her."

Beatrice, her face set with determination, asked, "How do we fight something that exists within a network, something that isn't bound by physical form?"

Selene's eyes glinted with fierce resolve. "We must disrupt his control over technology, expose his manipulations, and rally others to our cause. The Aeon Tear Stone now within this necklace can help us communicate and coordinate our efforts. We must also harness the knowledge and power of the ancient guardians, the wolves, who have fought against Morghast's influence for so long."

Chico, sat proudly on the back of the chair, chattered in agreement, while the wolves growled softly, their eyes reflecting their readiness for battle.

Selene's expression grew even more somber as she continued, her voice laden with the gravity of their situation.

"Morghast's influence goes beyond just manipulating technology. He has systematically undermined the very fabric of human society. People no longer engage in real communication with each other; instead, they interact through screens, their connections shallow and devoid of true emotion. This isolation breeds loneliness and despair, emotions upon which Morghast thrives."

Beatrice and Evelyn listened intently, their faces reflecting a mixture of shock and determination.

"The effects on people's health have been devastating," Selene continued. "Mental health issues have skyrocketed, with anxiety and depression becoming rampant. Physical health has also deteriorated as people become more sedentary and disconnected from the natural world. The sense of community and togetherness that once bound humanity has been eroded."

Selene gestured to the wolves, their eyes glowing with understanding and shared purpose. "The church, once a bastion of faith and hope, has been undermined as well. People no longer pray or believe in anything greater than themselves. Morghast has sown seeds of doubt and cynicism, turning people away from spirituality and faith. The sacred spaces of worship are now empty, their power diminished."

Evelyn's eyes widened with horror. "So, he's destroyed more than just technology. He's destroyed belief and trust."

Selene nodded. "Yes. Some call the constant flood of information propaganda or fake news, but these are just tools Morghast uses to control individuals. He manipulates information to create confusion and mistrust, breaking down societal cohesion. His network has even created new viruses, originally intended to kill good technology that could have opposed him. These technological viruses have now evolved into biological ones, infiltrating governments and being used to create real viruses that control the minds of humans."

Beatrice gasped, the enormity of the situation dawning on her. "You mean these viruses are designed to control people and disrupt society?"

"Exactly," Selene confirmed. "These biological viruses are engineered to target the human mind, sowing chaos, imprisoning people in their own homes, weakening resistance, and forcing the acceleration of technology into everyone's homes. They have also been used to take control of financial systems, causing economic instability and further breaking down societal structures. Morghast's goal is to create a world where he has absolute control, where individuals are isolated, distrustful, and easily manipulated."

Evelyn clenched her fists, her fear transforming into fierce resolve. "We can't let this continue. We have to fight back."

Beatrice, her face set with determination, placed a reassuring hand on Evelyn's shoulder. "We will. With Selene's guidance, the knowledge of the wolves, and the power of the Aeon Tear Stone, we can stand against Morghast's darkness."

Selene took a deep breath, her eyes filled with both gratitude and concern. "I am truly grateful that you both are willing to join me in this fight," she began, her voice steady but tinged with a hint of vulnerability. "But I must be honest with you. I am not as strong as I would like to be. The strike that nearly took Venus's life was an act of pure evil—a concentrated electromagnetic pulse directed straight into her brain."

Evelyn's eyes filled with tears as she looked at Selene, who was now embodying Venus's spirit. "Will she be alright?" she asked, her voice trembling.

Selene nodded, though her expression remained serious. "Venus will recover, but it will take time. Her spirit is resilient, but the damage was severe. She will regain her full strength slowly and because of this my power is weak as I am healing her. Until then, we must rely on each other and the guidance of the wolves."

Beatrice, her face set with determination, asked, "What must we do next?"

"The wolves will guide us, but our journey will not be easy," Selene explained. "We must find the Guardians—ancient beings who hold the magical power of the ages. They are the keepers of profound wisdom and strength, and with their help, we can stand a chance against Morghast. The quest to find them will be long and arduous, but it is our only hope."

Evelyn, wiping away her tears, nodded resolutely. "We'll do whatever it takes. We can't let Morghast's darkness continue to spread."

Selene smiled, a mixture of gratitude and resolve in her eyes. "Together, we have a chance. With the wolves guiding us and the Guardians' power, we can confront this evil and reclaim the light for our world."

Beatrice, feeling the weight of the task ahead but also the strength of their united resolve, placed a reassuring hand on Evelyn's shoulder. "We are stronger together. Let's prepare for the journey. With unity and courage, we will find the Guardians and defeat Morghast's dark influence."

The wolves, sensing the renewed determination in the room, growled softly in agreement. Chico, rolled in excitement on the table.

Selene's exhaustion suddenly became evident. With a weary sigh, she announced, "I need to rest before we set off." Understanding the importance of allowing Venus time to recuperate as well, the decision was made to take a brief respite at Evelyn's cottage.

Selene, with a gentle smile, laid down in front of the crackling fire and closed her eyes. With a soft shimmer of magic, her form began to shift and change until she took on the appearance of Venus, the French Bulldog.

Beatrice, sensing the need for some final preparations, announced that she would go and gather some supplies and pack a bag for the journey. Evelyn nodded in understanding, expressing her gratitude for Beatrice's help.

"Take your time, Beatrice. We'll make sure everything's ready here," Evelyn said, her voice soft with concern.

Beatrice smiled reassuringly. "Don't worry, Evelyn. I'll be back before dusk. We'll make sure we're well-prepared for the journey ahead."

With a nod of farewell, Beatrice bid them goodbye, Chico following close behind as they left the cottage.

The wolves remained steadfast, their watchful eyes scanning the surroundings as they stood guard outside the cottage.

The Alpha wolf's deep, commanding voice cut through the stillness of the forest, addressing Venus directly through the open doorway. "We'll keep watch while you rest, Venus," it said with a tone of authority and reassurance. Only Venus, in her canine form, understood the words clearly. To Evelyn, they sounded like a low growl, sending shivers down her spine. Venus, in her canine form, opened her one eye and gave a tired but appreciative woof before settling back down by the fire.

Feeling a little uneasy, Evelyn closed the front door behind her with trembling hands. The rustling of leaves and faint howls echoed in the distance as the wolves settled into their positions outside, standing guard for their safety.

Inside, the warmth of the fire enveloped the cottage in a sense of peace and safety, a brief respite before the journey ahead. The room soon filled with the gentle snores of Venus, a comforting sound amidst Evelyn's preparations.

Chapter 4 – 'The Quest Begins'

As night descended upon Evergreen City, the stars twinkled in the velvet sky, casting a soft glow over the tranquil forest. The wolves maintained their vigilant watch outside Evelyn's cottage, their eyes gleaming with fierce protectiveness.

Beatrice returned with Chico the monkey just as the last rays of sunlight faded from the horizon, her arms laden with supplies and a bag slung over her shoulder. As she entered the cottage, Evelyn greeted her with a weary smile.

"Welcome back, Beatrice. I hope your trip was fruitful," Evelyn said, her voice carrying a note of exhaustion.

Beatrice nodded, setting down her belongings with a gentle thud. "Yes, I managed to gather everything we'll need for the journey ahead. How is Venus?" she asked, concern evident in her voice.

"Venus woke briefly earlier," Evelyn added, her voice soft as she watched the slumbering dog. "She ate a bit of food and drank some water, but she's clearly still exhausted. I think it's best to let her rest undisturbed for now."

Beatrice nodded in understanding, her gaze lingering on Venus with a mixture of concern and affection. "Agreed. Let's ensure she gets the rest she needs," she said gently, acknowledging the importance of allowing Venus to recuperate fully.

With a weary but determined sigh, Evelyn rose from her chair and approached Venus, placing a fresh bowl of water and a plate of food within her reach. Venus stirred briefly at the sound of Evelyn's footsteps, her stubby tail wagging weakly in acknowledgment before she drifted back into a peaceful slumber.

Chico, understanding the gravity of the situation, climbed down from the chair and settled himself close to Venus. He curled up beside her, his tiny hands resting gently on her fur, his eyes vigilant and alert. The monkey's posture was a clear message: he was determined to guard her through the night.

"We'll keep an eye on her throughout the night," Evelyn reassured Beatrice, her voice filled with a quiet resolve. "And in the morning, we'll be ready to continue our journey with renewed strength and determination."

Beatrice smiled gratefully, appreciating Evelyn's steadfast commitment to their mission and the well-being of their beloved companion. "Thank you, Evelyn. We'll rest well tonight and face whatever challenges come our way tomorrow, together."

"We must not forget our loyal guardians outside," Beatrice remarked, a thoughtful expression crossing her features. "I brought some meat from the village. I'll go and feed the wolves."

Evelyn nodded in agreement, grateful for Beatrice's consideration. "That's a good idea. They've been standing watch for hours," she replied, her voice tinged with appreciation.

Beatrice stepped outside into the cool night air, the sounds of the forest enveloping her in a comforting embrace. The wolves greeted her with a low rumble of recognition, their eyes bright with anticipation as she approached.

With practiced hands, Beatrice distributed the meat among the wolves, watching as they devoured it eagerly. "Thank you for your vigilance, my friends," she said softly, her voice carrying a hint of reverence. "Rest well tonight. We'll need your strength tomorrow."

The wolves, their bellies full and their spirits renewed, settled back into their positions, their eyes never straying from the cottage as they resumed their watch. With a final nod of acknowledgment, Beatrice rejoined Evelyn inside.

As the fire crackled softly in the hearth and the wolves maintained their watchful vigil outside, the two women settled in for the night, finding solace in each other's company and the knowledge that they were not alone in their quest. And as Venus slept peacefully by the fire, under the guard of Chico the monkey, her gentle snores filling the room, they drifted off to sleep, their dreams filled with visions of the challenges and triumphs that awaited them on their journey.

As the first light of dawn painted the sky with hues of pink and gold, signaling the beginning of a new day, the group stirred from their rest inside Evelyn's cottage. Venus, who had transformed into the mysterious woman Selene during the night, now stood by the fire, her demeanor serene and her expression resolute. She was already magically dressed in a flowing white dress, her presence commanding attention as she exuded an air of quiet strength.

With a sense of determination, Evelyn and Beatrice rose from their makeshift beds, ready to face the challenges that lay ahead. They exchanged a wordless glance, their eyes filled with a shared resolve, before turning their attention to the task at hand.

Beatrice approached Selene gently, a mixture of awe and concern in her eyes. "How are you feeling?" she inquired, her voice soft with concern.

Selene nodded, a small smile playing at the corners of her lips. "I am ready to face whatever lies ahead," she replied, her voice steady and unwavering.

Meanwhile, Evelyn tended to the wolves outside, ensuring they were well-fed and ready for the journey ahead. The wolves greeted her with eager whines and wagging tails, their loyalty unwavering as they prepared to accompany their human companions on the quest. The monkey Chico, with a mischievous glint in its eyes, chattered excitedly as it leaped onto the back of the Alpha wolf, settling into a comfortable position.

"We're all set," Beatrice announced, rejoining Evelyn inside the cottage. "The wolves are ready, and Selene seems prepared for the journey."

Evelyn nodded, the tension of the impending journey etched into the lines of her face. "Then we best be off," she murmured, casting her gaze over the quaint little cottage one last time before stepping firmly towards the unknown.

As if on cue, Selene emerged from the cottage, the morning light casting a delicate glow around her. Her eyes met Beatrice's and Evelyn's with an inscrutable calm as she declared in a resonating voice that seemed to ripple through the very heart of the forest, "Yes, the time has come to start this battle. It cannot wait any longer."

With those words hanging in the crisp morning air, Selene turned and locked eyes with the Alpha. A connection sparked between them, a communication transcending mere words. It was as if a whisper of an ancient language passed between them, leaving an immediate understanding in its wake.

Selene then turned to Evelyn and said, "The wolves say we head north through the dark forest, and we must hurry."

Her words echoed through the clearing, and the wolves responded with immediate action. The pack fell into formation behind their Alpha, their ears pricked and alert for any sign of danger that might lurk within the dense foliage. Chico, still perched atop the Alpha's back, chattered in excited anticipation.

Evelyn watched as Beatrice quickly gathered their meager supplies—a few loaves of freshly baked bread, a small wheel of hard cheese, fruits preserved in honey, and jars of fresh water from the stream that flowed by the cottage. Beatrice also made sure to grab a bag of medicinal herbs and poultices, just in case things took a turn for the worse. Evelyn herself strapped on her quiver filled with arrows and her trusted longbow.

However, when they turned to Selene, they saw she carried no bundle of supplies, no weapon for self-defense. There was nothing but the white dress upon her person and a strange amulet hanging around her neck that glinted peculiarly under the sun's early rays. It was an odd sight, and both Beatrice and Evelyn shared a glance of unease.

"Are you not going to carry anything for the journey?" Evelyn asked tentatively, trying not to sound too confrontational. She gestured to the provisions and weapons they had gathered.

There was a pause as Selene regarded them, a soft smile on her lips as if she was privy to some secret they were not. "I carry what I need," she replied cryptically. Her gaze fell onto the amulet around her neck, her fingers tracing over its smooth surface thoughtfully. "This is my defense and my sustenance."

Beatrice frowned but refrained from further questions. Somehow, even though she didn't completely understand, she trusted Selene. The woman had a way of commanding respect, her calm demeanor and unwavering belief in their cause sparking a similar faith within Beatrice.

"Then we should all remember to carry what we need," Beatrice responded.

With a sense of determination, they gathered their meager belongings and stepped out into the crisp morning air. The chill bit at their skin, awakening their senses and sharpening their focus. The wolves, with the monkey perched atop the Alpha wolf's back, seemed to understand their purpose and led the way as they set off on foot, their footsteps resounding through the forest like a drumbeat. Each step brought them deeper into uncharted territory, the unknown looming around every corner.

As they journeyed further into the unexplored wilderness, the terrain grew increasingly rugged and treacherous. Their once well-defined path was now a maze of tangled roots and thick underbrush, testing their endurance and agility as they carefully navigated through the dense foliage. Every step required careful consideration, as one wrong move could lead to injury or worse. But undeterred by the challenges ahead, they pressed on, determined to reach their destination no matter what obstacles lay in their path.

Evelyn wiped the sweat from her brow, her breath coming in short gasps as she struggled to keep pace with the wolves. "I don't know how much longer I can keep this up," she admitted, her voice tinged with exhaustion.

Beatrice nodded in agreement; her brow furrowed with concern. "It seems the journey is taking its toll on all of us; age is catching up with me," she remarked.

Meanwhile, Selene floated gracefully through the forest, her movements seemingly effortless compared to the tired strides of her human companions. Despite the physical strain of the journey, there was an otherworldly serenity about her, as if she were untouched by the fatigue that plagued the others.

"Evelyn, Beatrice, are you both alright?" Selene's voice floated through the air like a gentle breeze, her concern visible as she glanced back at her companions.

Evelyn offered a weary smile, her eyes reflecting a mixture of gratitude and exhaustion. "We're hanging in there, thanks to your guidance," she replied, her voice tinged with relief.

Beatrice nodded in agreement, her eyes flickering with admiration as she observed Selene's graceful movements. "You seem to glide through the forest as if it were nothing," she remarked, a hint of awe in her voice.

Selene smiled warmly, her gaze shifting to the animals that now awaited them in the clearing. "I am merely following the path that the forest lays before me," she replied, her voice filled with humility. "But I am aware of the strain it puts on you both, and I am grateful for your resilience."

Meanwhile, the wolves, sensing their humans' struggle, conferred among themselves in low, guttural growls. Their keen instincts told them that a solution was needed to alleviate the strain of travel.

"It's no use pushing ourselves to exhaustion," one of the wolves rumbled to Selene, its voice deep and resonant. "We need a different approach if we're to continue."

Selene reassured Evelyn and Beatrice, "The wolves understand that you are exhausted, but they insist that we cannot stop yet. They are determined to find a solution. I have complete faith in them; after all, they are incredibly intelligent creatures."

The pack of six wolves stood in silent agreement, their ears pricked and their nostrils flaring as they prepared to set off into the surrounding forest. Each step was taken with stealth and precision, their senses attuned to the slightest rustle of leaves or snap of a twig. As they disappeared into the dense foliage, their coats blended seamlessly with the shadows, making them almost invisible to any unsuspecting prey. The hours ticked by, but finally they returned, their muzzles stained with dirt and their eyes glinting with a fierce determination that could only come from a successful hunt.

"We've found a solution," the Alpha wolf announced, its voice filled with confidence. "Selene, follow us."

Selene instructed Evelyn and Beatrice to follow the wolves. Eager to see what the wolves had discovered; Evelyn and Beatrice followed their furry guides deeper into the forest. As they emerged into a small clearing, they were met with an unexpected sight—three large animals, herded up like sheep, stood waiting for them.

Evelyn's eyes widened in surprise as she took in the scene before her. "What on earth are those?" she asked, her voice filled with wonder.

Beatrice chuckled softly, a smile playing at the corners of her lips. "It seems our furry friends have found us some transportation," she replied, her eyes twinkling with amusement.

The animals in question were a terrifying crew—three wild stallions stood before them, with an angry demeanor, they were kicking and stomping the ground. The tallest horse reared up onto its front legs and tried to kick out with its front legs. They looked dangerous, and far too fierce for any rider.

As Evelyn and Beatrice approached the majestic creatures, Selene stepped forward, her presence commanding attention. With a sense of purpose, she raised her hands, her necklace glowing with an otherworldly light as she began to recite ancient words in a melodious chant:

"Anima magna, aurum lucis,

Pax et amicitia inter nos creet,

Corpora nostra sint in armonia,

Et viam nobis monstrare dignare."

As Selene spoke, a sense of tranquility washed over the clearing, and the stallions responded to her words with a gentle nod of their heads. The once wild and angry horses now stood before them with a relaxed stance, and the tallest horse nuzzled Selene's outstretched hand, its eyes filled with trust. Magical saddles, shimmering with enchantments, appeared on each of the horses, ready to carry their new riders on their quest.

With a smile of satisfaction, Selene turned to Evelyn and Beatrice. "They will now be responsive to all of us," she explained, her voice filled with assurance. "Let us embark on our journey together."

"Well, I suppose it beats walking," Evelyn remarked, a hint of relief in her voice as she approached her horse.

Beatrice nodded in agreement, her excitement building as she eyed the horse with anticipation. "Let's mount up and see where these creatures take us," she suggested, her voice filled with enthusiasm.

With a mixture of excitement and trepidation, Evelyn and Beatrice mounted their respective stallions, the wolves leading the way as they set off once more. The journey had taken an unexpected turn, but with their newfound companions by their side, they were ready to face whatever challenges lay ahead.

As they traveled, Evelyn couldn't help but notice how serene and focused Selene remained. Despite the arduous journey, she seemed untouched by fatigue. "Selene, how do you stay so strong?" Evelyn asked, her voice filled with genuine curiosity.

Selene's gentle smile remained as she gazed ahead. "My inner strength is rooted in my connection with the ancient forces that guide us. But I also recognize your struggles, and I appreciate your perseverance."

The day wore on, and the group's progress continued steadily. As the sun began to dip below the horizon, casting long shadows across the forest floor, the wolves led them to a secluded clearing. It was a perfect spot to rest, with a gentle stream providing fresh water and soft moss offering a comfortable place to sleep.

"We'll camp here for the night," Selene announced, her voice carrying a note of authority. "We all need our rest if we are to continue our journey tomorrow."

As they dismounted and began to set up camp, Beatrice approached Evelyn, her eyes filled with a mixture of concern and determination. "We need to be ready for whatever lies ahead. This journey is just beginning, and we have many challenges to face."

Evelyn nodded, her resolve strengthening. "We'll face them together, with Selene and the wolves by our side. We're stronger than we think."

With the fire crackling and the wolves standing guard, the group settled down for the night. Selene transformed back into Venus, her small form curling up by the fire, her gentle snores filling the night air. Beatrice and Evelyn exchanged a final, reassuring glance before settling down to sleep, knowing that they were on the right path, guided by ancient magic and the unbreakable bond of their newfound companionship.

Chapter 5 – 'The First Attack'

As the first light of dawn crept through the trees, Venus stirred quietly from her place by the fire. Transforming from Venus into Selene's human form, she moved with unnatural grace, her white dress fluttering like a whisper in the morning breeze. Her necklace glowed softly, a source of her immense power.

Selene extended her hands, murmuring ancient words of magic.

"Cibus magicae, lux matutina, dona nobis fortitudinem."

As she spoke, the ingredients for breakfast appeared before her: freshly baked bread, wild berries, and a savory stew simmering in a pot. She orchestrated the meal with a mere flick of her wrist, the food arranging itself on wooden plates and bowls. Then, with a flick of her fingers, she summoned a feast for the wolves: a generous spread of roasted meats—deer, rabbit, and wild boar—laid out on a wooden platter.

With the feast prepared, Selene returned to her canine form. As Venus, she padded gently around the camp, nudging each of her companions awake with a gentle nuzzle. "You all must eat," she barked softly, her eyes conveying a mixture of warmth and urgency.

With a loud stretch and a jaw-cracking yawn, Evelyn's eyes flew open at the sight of the sumptuous feast laid out before them. "Good morning, Venus!" she exclaimed, her voice filled with astonishment and joy. "You can speak? My god, this is incredible." Her gaze swept over the mouthwatering spread before her, realizing that her companion had prepared it all. "Did you really do all of this, Venus? It looks absolutely amazing."

Venus spoke up once more. "No, Selene made this for you. I told her that if you don't eat in the morning, you get very grumpy." Evelyn burst into laughter and embraced Venus tightly. Venus snuggled back against her owner and let out a contented grunt. Then she waddled over to a bowl filled with food, and happily ate while grunting some more. After quenching her thirst with water, Venus settled down by Evelyn.

Beatrice nodded in agreement, her stomach rumbling in anticipation. "Selene has outdone herself, I am starving" she added, taking a seat by the fire.

As everyone gathered around the fire to eat, Selene transformed from Venus once again. The energy in the clearing shifted as her peaceful and comforting presence took over. The wolves eagerly consumed their meal, their eyes shining with contentment as they tore into the cooked meats. Selene spoke up, "Venus wanted to see you both, she talks to me all the time. She is still recovering, and she says she spoke to you for the first time. This is wonderful news; it means she is beginning to tap into her inner magic."

Evelyn's expression shifted from surprise to disbelief, her eyes wide and mouth agape as she struggled to comprehend what Selene had just revealed. "Magic? Venus?" she exclaimed in shock. Selene's voice took on a grave tone as she explained further, "Yes, magic flows within us all, but only a select few can truly harness its power. And Venus, she has the potential to become one of the most powerful wielders of magic I've ever seen." Unable to contain her curiosity any longer, Evelyn blurted out the question burning in her mind since they began their perilous journey together. "But where are we going next, Selene? What dangers lie ahead for us?"

Selene smiled, her eyes reflecting the fire's warm glow. "Our next destination is the ancient Temple of the Guardians," she explained. "Within its sacred walls lies the Codex Aetheris, an ancient tome that holds the spells necessary to recall the Guardians. These spirits are our guides and protectors, beings of immense power who can aid us in the battle against the dark forces."

Evelyn listened intently, her curiosity piqued. "What role do the Guardians play?" she asked.

Selene's expression grew serious as she continued. "The Night Spirits are ancient beings, each embodying a different aspect of nature and magic. They are the bearers of wisdom, strength, and guidance. When summoned, they can provide us with the knowledge and power we need to confront the evil that has taken hold of our world."

Beatrice leaned forward, her eyes shining with interest. "And the Temple of the Guardians—why is it so important?"

"The Temple of the Guardians is a place of great significance," Selene replied. "It is where the ancient guardians of the world once resided, and it holds the accumulated wisdom and magic of generations. The Codex Aetheris is kept there, protected by powerful wards and enchantments. It is the only place where we can find the spells to summon the Guardians, from their banishment."

She paused, then added, "The Guardians are the only ones who can track the true source of our enemy's power. The wolves, with all their keen senses and bravery, can only do so much. The dark magician who controls the network has hidden his true location well, masking his presence with powerful spells and dark magic. Only the Night Spirits possess the ability to see through these deceptions and lead us to him."

Evelyn and Beatrice exchanged determined glances, their resolve strengthening. "Then we must reach the temple," Evelyn said firmly. "Whatever it takes."

Selene nodded; her gaze unwavering. "Indeed. The journey will be perilous, but with the help of the wolves and our combined strength, we have a chance. The temple is hidden deep within the forest, guarded by ancient magic and the spirits of the guardians themselves. We must be prepared for anything."

As they finished their breakfast, Selene explained further. "I do not need food for sustenance," she said, her eyes glowing softly. "I rely on magic for my life force, which comes from the necklace around my neck. However, Venus needs her strength and is still recovering."

With their spirits lifted and their journey made easier by the hearty meal, the group set off toward the ancient temple, their hearts filled with hope and determination.

The sun climbed higher in the sky as the group traveled through the dense forest, its rays piercing through the canopy and creating a mosaic of light and shadow on the forest floor. The heat was stifling, and the wolves panted heavily, their tongues lolling as they struggled to keep cool.

Selene, ever perceptive, noticed their discomfort. "We need to find water," she said, her voice carrying a note of concern. "The wolves are thirsty, and we all could use a break."

Evelyn and Beatrice nodded in agreement, their own throats parched. They pressed on, guided by the wolves' keen senses, until they came upon a clearing bathed in the golden light of the mid-morning sun. At the center of the clearing lay a pristine lake, its surface shimmering like a mirror. The sight was a welcome relief.

But something strange and out of place caught their attention. By the edge of the still, reflective lake, a figure dressed in vibrant red danced and twirled, seemingly oblivious to the wild surroundings. As they drew closer, they saw that it was a woman with short black hair, her high heels sinking into the soft ground as she moved. Her makeup was heavily applied, completely out of place for daytime. Despite the untamed wilderness surrounding her, she had no bag or supplies with her and seemed completely unprepared for the rugged environment.

The wolves wasted no time, bounding towards the lake to quench their thirst. Selene, Evelyn, and Beatrice dismounted their magnificent horses and approached the woman cautiously. She was singing loudly into a small device attached to a stick, which she waved around with dramatic flair. She seemed completely unaware of the pack of wild wolves close by, as well as horses. Her eyes were fixed on the device, lost in her own choreographed performance.

"Is she... live streaming?" Evelyn asked, incredulous.

Selene was equally perplexed. "What is this dark magic before us?" she murmured, her eyes narrowing as she took in the strange scene.

"Excuse me," Selene called out, stepping forward. "Are you alright?"

The woman turned sharply, her expression one of annoyance. "I'm busy!" she snapped. "Can't you see I'm live streaming to my fans?" She pointed to her phone, which was propped up on a selfie stick.

Selene raised an eyebrow. "Live streaming? Out here?"

The woman rolled her eyes. "Yes, obviously. My fans love it. They would love that eye patch too," she added, pointing at Selene's accessory. "Where did you get it? My followers are always looking for new fashion tips."

Evelyn and Beatrice exchanged bewildered glances. The woman continued without waiting for an answer. "You're ruining my stream. My Yik Yok followers demand constant entertainment. If I don't sing and dance, they'll lose interest. Do you know how many followers I have? I'm Sapphire, by the way. You should follow me."

Selene's perplexity turned to concern. "Do you realize you're in the middle of a dangerous forest? There are wild animals, and you're... performing like this?"

Sapphire scoffed, flipping her hair dramatically. "Dangerous? Please. I have over a million followers. Nothing can touch me. I have to keep them engaged or I'll lose my influence. You wouldn't understand."

Selene's expression grew grave. "This is worse than I thought," she said, mostly to herself. "You're lost and don't even realize it. You're endangering your life to maintain popularity with people you'll never meet."

Sapphire seemed unfazed, adjusting her phone for a better angle. "You're ruining my shot," she repeated, resuming her dancing and singing. "Go away if you're not going to join in."

Evelyn shook her head in disbelief. "She's completely under the influence of the dark forces, isn't she?"

Selene nodded slowly. "Yes. This poor soul is caught in the web of the network's control, performing like a circus animal for a faceless audience. It's a powerful enchantment, one that traps people in a cycle of seeking validation and approval."

Beatrice sighed, her heart heavy with empathy. "We need to move on. There's nothing we can do for her now."

As they turned to leave, Sapphire called out, "Don't forget to follow Sapphire_Star on Yik Yok! You won't regret it!"

The group moved back into the forest, the strange encounter weighing heavily on their minds. Selene's eyes were filled with determination. "This just proves how insidious our enemy is. We must reach the Temple of the Guardians and find the Codex Aetheris. The Night Spirits are our only hope to uncover the true source of this evil and put an end to it."

Evelyn and Beatrice shared a determined glance, their jaws set and muscles tense. Without a word, they remounted their horses and urged them forward, following the path laid out by the wolves. The forest closed in around them, suffocating and ominous, but they pushed through, their hearts heavy with the weight of countless lives depending on their success.

As the group continued their journey through the dense forest, an uneasy silence settled over them. The sun cast dappled shadows on the ground, but the beauty of the scene was marred by an undercurrent of tension. The birds had ceased their songs, and even the wind seemed to hold its breath.

Selene led the way, her steps light and purposeful, her white dress flowing like a ghostly presence. Evelyn and Beatrice followed close behind, mounted on their proud stallions, their eyes darting nervously to the shadows between the trees. The wolves flanked them, their ears perked and their senses on high alert.

The small monkey shook with terror, its claws digging into the Alpha wolf's thick fur as if for dear life. Its wide, panicked eyes darted frantically, scanning for any sign of danger. The wolves snarled and snapped at each other sensing danger around them, their sharp teeth bared in a primal display of dominance. Through it all, the monkey clung on desperately, its heart beating so fast it felt like it might burst out of its chest.

Evelyn leaned forward, whispering to Beatrice. "Something's not right. The forest feels... different. Do you hear that?"

Beatrice nodded, her grip tightening on the reins of the stallion. "Yes, I do. It's too quiet. And the monkey is clearly terrified. We need to stay vigilant."

Suddenly, a sharp crack echoed through the forest, the sound of a branch breaking underfoot. The group halted, their hearts pounding. Selene raised a hand, signaling for silence. Her eyes scanned the surrounding trees, her senses reaching out to detect any magical disturbances.

"What was that?" Evelyn whispered, her voice barely audible.

"I don't know," Beatrice replied, her voice trembling slightly. "But we need to be prepared for anything."

The wolves sniffed the air, their hackles raised. The Alpha wolf growled, a warning to whatever was lurking in the shadows. The monkey let out a fearful screech, burying its face in the wolf's fur.

"We're not alone," Selene said quietly, her voice steady. "Something is following us, and it's getting closer."

Evelyn tightened her grip on the reins, her eyes darting around the forest. "What should we do?"

"Stay close and keep moving," Selene instructed. "We need to find a safe place to regroup and figure out what's following us."

As they resumed their journey, the sense of unease grew stronger. Strange noises filled the air—rustling leaves, snapping twigs, and the occasional distant howl. The wolves stayed close, their eyes scanning the forest for any sign of danger.

After what felt like hours of tense travel, Selene raised her hand again, signaling for the group to stop. "We need to confront whatever is following us," she said, her voice firm. "We can't keep running forever."

The group dismounted their horses, forming a protective circle. Selene stood at the center, her necklace glowing with a soft, pulsing light. She began to chant in the ancient tongue, her voice rising and falling like the wind through the trees.

"Ego voco te, spiritus silvae, manifestare et revelare inimicum nostrum."

The air around them seemed to shimmer, and a faint glow appeared in the distance. The strange noises grew louder, closer, until they could see shapes moving through the trees. Shadows darted between the trunks, swift and menacing.

"Be ready," Selene warned, her eyes fixed on the approaching forms. "Whatever it is, we must face it together."

The fierce wolves bared their sharp, glistening teeth, growling with primal aggression that made Evelyn and Beatrice's blood run cold. They cautiously inched forward, their weapons gripped tightly—a kitchen knife glinting in Evelyn's trembling hand, a last-minute choice now proving to be a lifeline, while Beatrice held out her bow with arrows drawn for action. The air was thick with tension and fear, their hearts pounding in unison as they braced for the inevitable clash. The small monkey huddled against the fearsome Alpha wolf, its pitiful whimpers drowned out by the deafening sound of adrenaline coursing through their veins. Their survival instincts kicked into high gear as they prepared to face off against these formidable predators.

As the shadows closed in, the group stood firm, united by their determination and the bond they shared. They knew that whatever awaited them, they would face it together, ready to fight for their lives and the fate of the world.

Selene, her necklace glowing with a soft, pulsing light, began to chant in the ancient tongue, her voice rising and falling like the wind through the trees.

"Ego voco te, virtus aeternum, manifesta et protege."

The shadows seemed to dance and flicker as they approached, their forms indistinct but undeniably menacing. The air grew colder, a chill seeping into their bones as the creatures drew nearer. Evelyn and Beatrice exchanged nervous glances, their hands trembling but resolute. The wolves, standing shoulder to shoulder, let out a collective growl, their eyes glowing with fierce determination.

Selene's chanting grew louder, her voice a beacon of strength and power. The necklace around her neck pulsed with a radiant light, casting an eerie glow over the forest clearing. The shadows halted just at the edge of the light, their movements erratic and restless.

"Evelyn, Beatrice," Selene called out, her voice carrying an authoritative tone. "Stand ready. These are not mere beasts. They are manifestations of dark magic, sent to test our resolve."

Evelyn's fingers clenched around the cold, sharp blade of the kitchen knife, her knuckles turning white as she prepared to defend herself and the group. Beatrice shifted her stance, her eyes scanning their surroundings for any signs of danger. Every breath they took felt like a weight on their chests, the air thick with tension and fear. The slightest noise could send them into a frenzy, ready to fight for their lives against any threat that may come their way.

In one swift, fluid motion, a shadow seemed to detach itself from the darkness, lunging forward with unnatural speed. As it entered the light, it took on a solid form—a grotesque, snarling beast with razor-sharp teeth and claws. The Alpha wolf, sensing danger, leapt into action, meeting the creature head-on with a ferocious snap of its powerful jaws. The clash between these two formidable creatures was like a violent storm, fur flying and fangs bared as they fought for dominance in a flurry of primal instincts.

A wave of shadows surged forward, their dark shapes writhing and twisting in the moonlight. The pack of wolves, fierce and unyielding, met them head-on, snarling and baring their sharp teeth. The clearing became a battleground, chaotic and frenzied as the sounds of battle filled the air. Every blow was met with an otherworldly hiss or screech. The smell of blood and sweat mingled together, overpowering the sweetness of pine and earth that usually permeated the forest.

Selene's voice rose to a deafening pitch as she chanted, her hands trembling with raw power raised high above her head. A blinding barrier of light erupted from her palms, pushing back the horde of creatures with a force that shook the earth beneath them. Her eyes glowed with an otherworldly intensity, veins pulsing with ancient magic as she poured every ounce of energy into the spell. The air crackled with electricity and the ground trembled with each syllable she spoke, her voice resonating with a primal power that seemed to shake reality itself.

"Ego voco te, lumen divinum, defende nos ab obscuris animis."

The blinding light pulsated, searing through the darkness and forcing the shadows to retreat. The creatures, however, were undeterred, their relentless attacks overwhelming the wolves. As their strength began to dwindle, a deafening roar split through the air, drowning out the chaos of battle. It was a sound that struck fear into the hearts of both friend and foe alike.

From the depths of the forest emerged a formidable figure, its imposing presence filling the air with a sense of reverence and fear. It was a majestic Stag, its massive antlers adorned with shining runes that seemed to pulsate with power. Its piercing eyes glowed with an otherworldly intensity, daring any to challenge its authority. With a thunderous roar, a lone Guardian charged into battle, sending the shadowy creatures scattering in all directions. This was one of the legendary protectors they had been searching for—a being of immense strength and ancient wisdom.

The wolves, their fur matted and bloodied from the intense battle, let out triumphant howls as they caught sight of the Guardian. The majestic creature stood tall and proud, its antlers gleaming in the shadows of the woods. With newfound strength and determination, the wolves launched themselves at the shadowy figures. Their sharp teeth glistened in the dim light as they tore through the darkness, driving it back into the depths of the forest. The Alpha wolf, now standing side by side with the powerful stag, delivered a final ferocious blow that caused the remaining shadows to retreat into the night.

Breathing heavily, the group regrouped, their eyes wide with relief and disbelief. The Guardian stepped forward, its presence radiating strength and wisdom.

"Selene," it spoke in a deep, resonant voice, "you have summoned me in your time of need. I am the Guardian of the East, here to aid you in your quest."

Selene nodded, her exhaustion evident but her spirit unbroken. "Thank you, noble Guardian. We are in dire need of your assistance. We seek the Codex Aetheris, to summon the other Guardians. Only they can track the source of the dark magic that plagues our world."

The Guardian bowed its head in acknowledgment. "The path to the ancient temple is fraught with danger, but with my guidance, you will reach it. The Guardians will heed your call, for they are the only ones who can pierce the veil of darkness that hides our enemy."

A glimmer of hope sparked between Evelyn and Beatrice as they exchanged a meaningful glance, their spirits lifted by the words of the wise Guardian. The monkey, previously cowering in fear with its hands over its eyes, slowly relaxed and stared at the majestic Stag Guardian in awe. Its wide eyes seemed to reflect the wisdom and power of the ancient creature in front of them.

With a nod of recognition, the Guardian moved his enormous head in the direction of the wolves, their bodies still riddled with wounds. "Your brave warriors will need my assistance." He lowered his head and a soft light began to glow from the runes adorning his antlers.

"Curatio," he chanted, his voice resonating through the silence of the forest. With each syllable, the light from the antlers intensified until it shone with the brightness of a thousand moons. The light then slowly descended, enveloping each wolf in a warm, healing aura. Every wound began to visibly mend itself; fur regrew in place of bare skin, torn flesh stitched together to become whole once more.

As if borne by an eternal wind, Selene's necklace lifted gently off her chest, answered by the stag's beckoning magic. It pulsed brightly in response to the Guardian's ancient incantation, casting an array of lights that danced around her like will-o'-the wisps. The luminescent colors mirrored the hues of the dawn—a spectacle that was both mesmerizing and humbling.

"Licentia," Selene whispered, her voice barely audible. The power radiating from her necklace amplified, responding to

her command. A gentle breeze stirred the stillness, its cool touch bringing relief and tranquility. The wolves whimpered as their pain receded, replaced with a comforting warmth that seemed to seep into their very bones.

As the spell's potency began to wane, the wolves stood up, their eyes glowing with renewed vigor and strength. Their once ragged fur now gleamed in rays of sunshine, reflecting their regained health and vitality. It was as if they had never been wounded before. They let out a series of howls that echoed throughout the forest, expressing gratitude for the gift they had received.

The Guardian of the East nodded approvingly at Selene who exhaled deeply, a slight smile gracing her lips. She looked at the wolves, her heart swelling with triumph and relief. "The power of healing lies within all of us," she said, her voice soft yet resonant in the stillness of the night. "And it is in unity and selfless sacrifice that our true strength is revealed."

Evelyn and Beatrice watched, their eyes filled with admiration and awe. Evelyn turned to Beatrice, her face illuminated by the soft glow from the rejuvenated wolves.

"We have come far, Bea," she murmured, "and we have much further to go."

"We'll make it," Beatrice replied confidently, her gaze unwavering as she faced the daunting darkness that lay ahead on their path. "Together."

The Guardian of the East regarded them carefully and then gestured his massive head towards the unbroken darkness that lay ahead. "The temple of Guardians awaits," he announced solemnly. "Prepare yourselves."

The monkey clambered up onto the Alpha Wolf while Evelyn, Beatrice, and Selene mounted their horses. The horses, also rejuvenated by the Guardian's healing magic, pranced with a renewed energy. The trio exchanged a glance of determination before nudging their steeds forward. The Guardian took the lead, with the Alpha wolf at his side. The wolves ran alongside the horses, forming a new united front for battle. The Guardian's voice echoed in their minds as they advanced, *"Lumen illius est via,"* he intoned. A radiant orb of light sprung from his antlers, illuminating the path ahead. Its glow shimmered on the damp earth, drawing long shadows that danced as they rode. The path bent and snaked like a winding river, framed by towering trees and thick ferns filled with unseen creatures of the dark wood.

Following the Guardian's lead, their horses picked up speed. Their hooves thudded rhythmically against the earthy trail, each step carrying them closer to their goal.

Selene turned to the group, her eyes filled with determination. "With the Guardian by our side, we have a fighting chance. Let us press on, for the fate of our world depends on it."

Chapter 6 – 'Forest Hunt'

As the sun began to set, the shadows around them deepened and stretched endlessly through the dense forest. Every step they took was accompanied by the sound of crunching leaves and twigs, as if the forest floor was alive beneath their feet. The Alpha wolf, with the majestic Stag by his side, led the way with a graceful yet cautious gait. His senses were alert to any signs of danger, his ears picking up on every rustle of leaves and snap of branches.

Evelyn and Beatrice followed closely behind, their eyes darting in all directions with apprehension. The wolves flanked them, their growls low and menacing, while the small monkey clung tightly to the Alpha wolf's back, its body trembling with fear. Evelyn's mind wandered to her childhood, recalling the time she had ventured too far into the woods near her home and encountered a mysterious old woman who had taught her the ways of herbs and healing. It was that encounter that had set her on the path to becoming a healer, using her knowledge to help those in her village.

Beatrice, on the other hand, was haunted by memories of the battles she had fought against the dark forces. She had lost loved ones and comrades, and the pain of those losses drove her to study ancient texts and magical tomes, seeking the power to prevent such tragedies from happening again. Her dedication had earned her a place among the most respected mages, but it had come at a heavy cost.

As they pressed deeper into the forest, it opened up into a clearing that seemed almost enchanted. In its center stood a massive, ancient tree whose gnarled roots twisted and turned, forming natural pathways and hidden alcoves. Its bark was knotted and rough, a testament to the countless years it had weathered. But what truly drew their attention were the symbols etched into the tree trunk. They were ancient, as old as time itself. Selene could feel a hum of power emanating from them and was inexplicably drawn towards it.

These symbols were not done by human hands but rather seemed to be the work of an unseen force, perhaps nature herself. Each symbol was unique, their lines varied in thickness and length, creating a weird sense of rhythm that was almost musical when gazed upon. They covered the entire tree, some nearly faded with time while others freshly inked by what seemed like a supernatural hand.

The air was thick with the scent of moss and earth, and a vibrant glow seemed to emanate from the very core of the ancient tree.

"We're close," Selene whispered, her voice barely audible above the rustling leaves. "The entrance to the ancient temple lies beyond this tree. We must proceed with caution."

Before they could take another step, a chilling howl pierced through the air, followed by heavy footsteps that seemed to shake the ground. The group froze in terror, their hearts pounding in unison.

"We can't outrun it," Beatrice murmured, her voice trembling. "Whatever it is, it's closing in on us."

Selene nodded solemnly, her eyes narrowing with determination. "Then we make our stand here. Prepare yourselves."

The wolves formed a protective circle around them, their menacing growls growing louder with each passing second. The small monkey let out a frightened screech, seeking refuge behind the Alpha wolf's massive form.

From the inky depths of the shadows emerged a monstrous figure, cloaked in an impenetrable darkness that seemed to devour all light around it. Its eyes glowed with a sickly green hue, like burning embers of malice, and its body was a grotesque fusion of shadow and flesh. It moved with a sinuous and predatory grace, each step causing the ground to shake with its sinister intent. Selene's heart pounded against her ribcage as she felt its unrelenting hunger fixated on her, sending shivers down her spine like icy tendrils of fear.

The once peaceful clearing was now a battleground. The monstrous beast's call had summoned a horde of black creatures, hundreds of them pouring out from the forest in a relentless wave. Their eyes glowed with malice, their movements swift and menacing. The ground seemed to tremble under their sheer numbers and malevolent intent.

The stag, with its antlers still glowing, turned to the group. "Run!" it commanded, its deep voice resonating with authority. "To the giant oak! Now!"

With determination burning in their hearts, the group sprang into a full sprint toward the towering ancient tree. Selene, dressed in flowing white fabric, led the charge with her long hair streaming behind her like a banner of victory. Evelyn and Beatrice followed closely behind, their loyal animal companions they rode upon matching their urgency as they bounded over roots and rocks.

The wolves, fierce and protective, ran at the sides of their human counterparts, their savage snarls serving as a constant warning to whatever danger may be advancing behind them.

As they approached the mighty oak, a shimmering blue wall manifested out of thin air, encircling the sacred temple grounds. The barrier pulsed with powerful energy, its purpose clear - to keep out any darkness that dared to encroach upon the holy sanctuary.

In response to this imminent threat, the stag's antlers glowed even brighter, ancient symbols etching themselves onto the bark of the tree as it prepared to defend its home.

"Keep going!" the stag urged, its voice a mix of desperation and command. "This is the gate entry. It will not stay open long!"

The ancient symbols etched into the bark of the tree glowed with an otherworldly energy, pulsing and humming in a mesmerizing rhythm. As if responding to the mystical call, a gate began to materialize within the trunk of the mighty tree, its edges shimmering and flickering as they formed a hazy portal. The group of adventurers, hearts pounding with excitement and fear, dashed towards the opening, their feet churning up dirt and leaves behind them.

But they were not alone in their pursuit. The snarling creatures followed close behind, their eyes glowing with malevolent intent. The sound of their snarls and howls filled the air, creating a deafening cacophony that echoed through the forest.

In the chaos and urgency of the chase, one of the wolves stumbled and fell to the ground. Its yelps of pain were quickly drowned out by the savage growls of the black creatures that descended upon it, tearing it apart with vicious claws and teeth. The haunting cries of the dying wolf reverberated through the trees, serving as a grim reminder of the deadly danger that pursued them.

Evelyn's scream tore from her throat, a desperate plea to save the fallen wolf. But urgency drowned out any chance of stopping as the gate loomed ahead, threatening to seal their fates. With all their might, they burst through just as it shimmered and began to shut. The stag, its antlers ablaze with determination, was the final one to cross the threshold, narrowly escaping certain doom.

As they stumbled through the gate, it sealed shut behind them with a deafening clang. The tree reformed with a sickening crunch.

The shimmering wall shielded them from the onslaught of black creatures. They slammed into the barrier, their twisted forms exploding into ash and smoke upon contact. The relentless horde pounded against the force field, unable to break through.

Gasping for air and trembling with terror, the group collapsed onto the ground, their eyes wide with shock and disbelief at the gruesome scene before them. The wolves circled protectively, growling low in their throats as they mourned the loss of one of their own.

"We made it," Beatrice gasped, her voice trembling with exhaustion and shock. "But that was too close."

Selene, her face pale but resolute, nodded. "This place is sacred. The symbols on the stag's antlers opened the gate. We are safe for now. We will travel on foot, the horses have done their job, they are free."

Evelyn, still reeling from the loss of the wolf, looked at Selene. "What were those things? How did they find us so quickly?"

"The dark magician's reach is vast," Selene explained, her voice heavy with sorrow. "His minions are many, and they are relentless. But we are here now, on the edge of the temple's protective grounds. This place is ancient and powerful. It will give us the time we need."

Evelyn's eyes welled up with fresh tears as she remembered the fallen wolf. The reality of their situation struck her with full force - they were alone in a place that was beautiful and deadly at the same time.

The stag's voice broke the brief silence, its tone filled with urgency. "We have no time to rest," it declared, its eyes fixed on the Alpha wolf. "I am deeply sorry for the loss of your pack member. Their sacrifice was not in vain."

The Alpha wolf raised its head, its eyes glistening with sorrow and determination. "Thank you," it growled softly. "But we cannot dwell on the loss. We must keep moving. The pack understands the dangers we face."

The stag nodded solemnly. "Your strength and resilience are commendable. We must press on if we are to stand a chance against the dark magician and his minions. Our journey to the ancient temple is vital. It holds the book that can summon the other Guardians, the only beings capable of tracking the source of the evil enemy. Without them, we are lost."

The Alpha wolf's eyes flickered with a mix of sadness and resolve. "We will do whatever it takes to ensure our mission succeeds. Our fallen comrade will be honored through our perseverance."

Selene stepped forward, placing a hand on the Alpha wolf's head. "Your bravery inspires us all. We move forward together, united in our purpose."

The Alpha wolf dipped its head in acknowledgment before turning to its pack. "Gather around," it commanded, its voice firm. The wolves formed a tight circle, their bodies close as they raised their heads to the sky. A mournful howl began, a haunting tribute to their lost member. The sound echoed through the temple grounds, a lament for the fallen and a vow of continued strength. As the wolves howled, the enemy continued to charge the shimmering wall.

Each creature that touched the barrier disintegrated instantly, turning to ash in a flash of blinding light. But their numbers were relentless. More surged from the forest, desperately trying to scale the protective wall, evaporating into ash as they touched it. The sight was both terrifying and awe-inspiring—a testament to the power of the dark magician's influence.

"We can't stay here much longer," Evelyn whispered, her voice filled with worry. "What if they find a way through?"

Beatrice placed a reassuring hand on her shoulder. "We won't let that happen. We'll find the ancient book, summon the Guardians, and put an end to this evil once and for all."

Selene's necklace glowed softly, a beacon of hope in the darkened forest. "We move now, and on foot," she said firmly. "Stay close, and stay vigilant." Evelyn, Beatrice, and Selene all dismounted their horses.

The group stepped forward, their eyes fixed on the ancient temple that loomed ahead. As they drew closer, the details of the sacred structure became clearer, and they marveled at the sight before them.

The temple was a grand edifice, its architecture a testament to a long-lost era. Majestic stone steps, worn smooth by countless years, led up to an imposing entrance framed by towering pillars. Each pillar was intricately carved with symbols and runes that glowed faintly in the dim light, telling stories of forgotten gods and ancient magic.

On either side of the entrance, torches burned with an otherworldly blue flame, casting an eerie yet inviting glow. The flames flickered and danced, their light reflecting off the polished stone and casting long shadows that seemed to move with a life of their own. The air was filled with the scent of incense and the faint hum of mystical energy.

As they ascended the steps, the group felt a sense of awe and reverence. The temple radiated a powerful aura, a sanctuary of ancient wisdom and protection. Selene led the way, her necklace pulsing in rhythm with the temple's energy, guiding them forward.

Upon reaching the top of the steps, they found themselves before a massive doorway, flanked by statues of guardians— figures of wolves, stags, eagles, and bears, their eyes seemingly alive with a vigilant presence. The door itself was made of heavy oak, bound with iron and inscribed with more of the glowing runes. "This place is incredible," Evelyn whispered, her voice filled with wonder. "You can feel the power here."

"Indeed," Selene replied, her eyes scanning the entrance. "The temple of the Guardians is a place of immense magical significance. Within its walls lies the Codex Aetheris —the Book of the Heavens. It holds the spells to summon all the Guardians, the only ones who can track the source of our enemy." Beatrice nodded, her hand resting on one of the guardian statues. "These statues...they're like sentinels. Protectors of the temple and its secrets."

Selene stepped forward, placing her hand on the door. Her necklace glowed brighter, and she began to chant in the ancient tongue, her voice resonating with the temple's energy.

"Porta sacra, aperi nobis, custodes antiqui, da nobis viam."

The door groaned and slowly swung open, revealing a grand hall lit by more of the blue-flamed torches. The interior was even more awe-inspiring—a vast space filled with ancient relics, tapestries depicting battles of old, and more statues of the sacred creatures. The ceiling was high and arched, adorned with murals of celestial scenes and mystical symbols.

At the far end of the hall stood an altar, and upon it lay a massive, leather-bound book. The Codex Aetheris. Its cover was decorated with silver inlays and intricate designs, and it seemed to hum with an ancient power.

"This is it," Selene said softly, her eyes fixed on the book. "The key to summoning the Guardians and finding the dark magician's true location."

The group moved forward, their footsteps echoing in the vast hall. The wolves remained alert, their eyes scanning the shadows for any signs of danger. The monkey, now calmer, clung to the Alpha wolf's back, its eyes wide with curiosity.

As they approached the altar, the air grew thick with anticipation. They knew that within these walls lay the answers they sought, the power they needed to combat the encroaching darkness. They prepared to unlock the ancient secrets of the temple and summon the Guardians to aid them in their quest.

As the group stepped forward, their eyes were drawn to the massive leather-bound book, the Codex Aetheris, resting on the altar. The sight of the ancient tome filled them with a mixture of awe and determination. Evelyn, curiosity piqued, turned to Selene with a question that had been gnawing at her mind.

"Selene," Evelyn began, her voice echoing softly in the grand hall, "why is it that the Stag Guardian is here with us, but the others are not? Shouldn't all the Guardians be here to protect this sacred place?"

Selene paused, her eyes lingering on the glowing symbols on the walls, before turning to face Evelyn. Her expression was somber, the weight of ancient knowledge heavy in her eyes.

"An ancient curse," Selene began, her voice filled with a mixture of sorrow and resolve, "was laid upon the Guardians by the Black Magician. This curse banished the other Guardians to distant realms, trapping them in a state of perpetual slumber. Only the Stag was able to escape the curse. He has been in hiding, waiting for the prophecy to be realized, for the chosen ones to come and lift the curse."

Beatrice, her hand still resting on one of the guardian statues, looked up with concern. "But why was the Stag able to escape when the others could not?"

Selene's eyes softened as she glanced at the majestic stag standing proudly beside them. "The Stag is unique among the Guardians. His connection to the ancient magic is stronger, and his willpower unmatched. He was able to resist the dark magic's grip long enough to find refuge. For centuries, he has awaited this moment, guided by the prophecy that foretold your arrival and the awakening of the Guardians."

The Stag, sensing the attention, lowered his head gracefully. "I have waited for this time, for the chosen ones to come and free my brethren," he said, his voice resonant and wise. "The prophecy spoke of a time when the darkness would rise once more, and only together could we stand against it."

Evelyn felt a surge of determination. "Then we must lift this curse and summon the other Guardians. We can't face the Black Magician alone."

Selene nodded, her eyes gleaming with resolve. "Exactly. The Codex Aetheris contains the spells we need to summon the Guardians and break the curse that binds them. With their help, we will have the power to confront the dark forces and restore balance."

The group moved closer to the altar, the wolves forming a protective circle around them. The monkey, still perched on the Alpha wolf's back, watched with wide eyes, its fear replaced by a growing sense of purpose.

As Selene reached out to open the Codex Aetheris, the ancient runes on the cover glowed brighter, responding to her touch. She began to chant once more, her voice blending with the hum of magical energy that filled the temple.

"Ancient spirits of the night, heed our call and join our fight. Break the chains that bind your might, and stand with us against the blight."

The air around them shimmered with magic, and the temple seemed to pulse with an ancient power.

As Selene's chanting echoed through the grand hall, the glowing runes on the Aertheris Book suddenly dimmed, and the book remained firmly shut. Confusion and frustration flickered across Selene's face. She tried once more, her voice growing louder and more urgent, but the ancient tome did not respond.

The Stag, observing the scene with a calm yet knowing expression, stepped forward. His antlers, still glowing faintly from the protective gate, cast a soft light on the book. "Selene," he said gently, his voice resonant and wise, "the prophecy speaks of Venus in her true form. Only she can unlock the Codex Aetheris. It is her destiny."

Selene's eyes widened in realization. "Of course," she whispered. The Stag continued, his voice carrying the weight of ancient wisdom. "The prophecy foretells of a dog with one eye, a creature of pure heart, who will be the light that brings balance to the world. Venus is that light. In her canine form, she is the key to unlocking the power we need."

Evelyn, spoke with a mixture of awe and determination. "Venus," she said softly, "you are our hope."

The Stag began to recite the ancient prophecy, his voice echoing through the temple:

"In a time of darkness, when shadows reign, A one-eyed dog shall break the chain. With a heart of gold and courage pure, She alone can find the cure.

In canine form, she holds the light, To banish darkness, bring back the night. Her single eye, a beacon bright, Will guide us through the endless fight.

From ancient times, this fate was sealed, Her power, the world's last shield. With her we stand, with her we fight, To restore the balance and make things right."

Selene spoke to Venus within herself, her voice filled with reverence. "Venus, you must cast the spell. Only you can awaken the Guardians and lift the curse."

Chapter 7 – 'Codex Aetheris'

Selene stood before the ancient Codex Aetheris, her white dress gleaming in the temple's ethereal light. As she focused on the necklace around her neck, it began to glow with an intense, radiant light, enveloping her entire body in a cocoon of magic. The gentle hum of the temple's energy filled the air, pulsing in rhythm with her heartbeat. Gradually, Selene's form started to shimmer and blur, dissolving into the sleek, loyal shape of Venus the dog. The transformation was swift yet graceful, a seamless merging of magic and flesh, casting a halo around her, emphasizing her singular, determined eye.

Venus, feeling the weight of her destiny, approached the Codex Aetheris with a sense of purpose. Her eye shone with determination as she turned to the Stag. "What should I do?" she asked, her voice steady but tinged with uncertainty.

The Stag, his eyes wise and ancient, replied, "Feel the power within yourself, Venus. You will know what to do."

Taking a deep breath, Venus closed her eye, focusing inward. She felt the magic of the necklace and the power coursing through her veins. As she embraced this inner strength, she began to rise, lifted by an invisible force. Hovering above the ground, she floated towards the altar, her paws outstretched towards the Codex Aetheris.

The ancient book responded to her presence, its pages flipping open to reveal a central parchment inscribed with arcane symbols. As Venus placed her paws on the book, the symbols began to glow, and a faint hum filled the air. The entire temple seemed to resonate with the power emanating from the Codex Aetheris.

Suddenly, ancient runes floated up from the pages of the book, swirling around the room in a mesmerizing dance. The runes glowed with a brilliant light, their shapes shifting and changing as they moved through the air. The entire temple was bathed in their radiant glow, casting intricate patterns on the walls.

With a deep, resonant voice, Venus began to call upon the Guardians. Her words, though ancient and powerful, flowed naturally from her:

"Custodes Aetheris, audite vocem meam,

Per lumen unius oculi,

Advenite ad nostram terram.

Ex umbris antiquis,

Surgite et nos defendite,

Virtutem vestram invoco,

Tenebras repellite."

The runes responded to her call, their light intensifying as they floated faster around the room. The air crackled with magical energy, and the temple seemed to vibrate with the power of the ancient words.

Venus hovered above the altar, her eye reflecting the glow of the ancient runes as they continued to swirl around the room. One by one, the Guardians began to materialize, each a unique embodiment of ancient power and wisdom. The air was thick with anticipation, and the temple's blue torchlight cast a shimmering glow as the Guardians appeared.

Guardian of the North: The Eagle

The Eagle soared down from above, its wings spreading wide as it landed gracefully beside the Stag. Its feathers were a brilliant mix of gold and white, and its eyes shone like twin suns. The runes on its body formed shapes of stars and celestial bodies, glowing with a radiant light. Around its neck, it wore a necklace of golden feathers, each one sparkling as if touched by the sun's rays.

Guardian of the South: The Giant Wolf

The Giant Wolf approached from a dark corner with silent, powerful strides, its silver-grey fur shimmering in the light. Its eyes were piercing blue, filled with a fierce determination. The runes on its body formed intricate patterns of waves and currents, glowing with a deep, azure light. Around its neck, it wore a chain of seashells and pearls, each one glistening like the ocean's depths.

Guardian of the West: The Brown Bear

The Brown Bear lumbered forward, appearing from a western wall. Its massive form exuding strength and resilience. Its fur was a rich, earthy brown, and its eyes were a warm, golden hue. The runes on its body formed symbols of mountains and earth, glowing with a steady, amber light.

Around its neck, it wore a necklace of polished stones, each stone emanating a warm, grounding energy.

Guardian of the East: The Stag

The Stag, already present and known to the group, stood majestically with its powerful antlers adorned with glowing symbols. Its eyes, deep and wise, radiated a sense of calm and protection. Around its neck, it now wore a chain of polished oak leaves, each one shimmering with a gentle, green light.

Venus, still hovering above the altar, felt the immense power and wisdom radiating from each Guardian. The ancient runes on their bodies pulsated in unison, creating a harmonious resonance that filled the temple.

As the last Guardian took its place, the room seemed to vibrate with the collective power of these ancient beings. Venus felt a deep connection to each one, understanding their roles and the strengths they brought to the fight against the dark forces.

With a steady, confident voice, Venus addressed the Guardians, "We stand united against the darkness that threatens our world. Your strength and wisdom are our guiding light. Together, we will bring balance and peace."

The Guardians bowed their heads in acknowledgment, their presence a powerful testament to the ancient prophecy being fulfilled. The temple, now filled with their radiant energy.

The Brown Bear, Guardian of the West, stepped forward, its massive form casting a formidable shadow. Rising onto its hind legs, it looked directly at Venus with fierce determination in its eyes.

"Venus," the Bear rumbled, its voice deep and resonant, "I thank you for bringing us here. For centuries, we have awaited this moment, bound by our duty and our promise. The Black Magician's name is a stain on our history, and I yearn for the chance to confront him, to avenge the pain he has inflicted on this world. His darkness has festered for too long, and I vow to fight him to the death."

The Bear's voice grew angrier as it spoke, each word dripping with the intensity of centuries-old rage. The temple seemed to tremble slightly, resonating with the Bear's powerful emotions.

Suddenly, the Eagle, Guardian of the North, appeared to enter a trance. Its eyes glazed over as it spoke in a voice that seemed to echo from another realm, "In order to travel and fight the Black Magician, we need human forms. We must possess the ability to move between our true forms and human-like forms to adapt to the challenges we will face."

The Giant Wolf, Guardian of the South, stepped forward next, its silver-grey fur glistening in the temple's light. "Venus," it said, its voice a soothing counterpoint to the Bear's anger, "only you can cast the spell that will enable us to occupy human forms that match our personalities. This transformation is essential for our quest. You must call upon the Codex Aetheris, our Book of Magic, and find the spell that will grant us this ability."

Venus nodded, feeling the weight of their request. She hovered closer to the altar, her gaze fixed on the ancient Codex Aetheris. The book, sensing her intent, began to flip open, its pages turning rapidly as if guided by an unseen hand. The sound of the pages flipping echoed through the temple, a rhythmic, almost hypnotic sound.

Finally, the book settled on a page, the ancient text glowing with golden light. Venus placed her paw on the parchment, feeling the surge of magic coursing through her. The runes around the room responded, floating in the air, shimmering with power.

Venus began to chant in the ancient tongue, her voice carrying the weight of millennia of knowledge and magic. The words flowed from her effortlessly, as if she had known them all her life.

"Forma humana,

da nobis potestatem,

ut inter mundos moveamus.

Magicae huius libri,

nos formam accipere iube.

Nos sumus custodes noctis,

adiuvare nos in proelio adveniente."

As she chanted, the runes glowed brighter, and a soft, pulsating light enveloped the Guardians. The Bear, Eagle,

Wolf, and Stag stood tall, their forms shimmering as the spell took hold. The air around them crackled with energy, and slowly, their animal forms began to blur, shifting and changing.

The Stag's transformation was the most elegant, shifting into an English gentleman. He wore a finely tailored suit complete with a top hat, exuding an air of noble dignity. His eyes retained the wise and gentle demeanor of his animal form, and his posture was straight and refined.

The Bear morphed into a strong, imposing Viking. With his muscular build and braided beard, he looked every bit the warrior of old. His eyes still burned with the fierce determination of his animal form, and his presence commanded respect and awe.

The Giant Wolf transformed into a Roman guard, complete with armor and a red-plumed helmet. His powerful frame and calm, authoritative demeanor reflected the strength and wisdom of his true form. His eyes, keen and perceptive, remained as vigilant as ever.

The Eagle's transformation was the most striking. She became a female pirate, with flowing black hair and a tricorn hat. Her attire was a mix of rugged and elegant, with a long coat and leather boots. Her sharp, piercing eyes still carried the regal authority of her eagle form, and she moved with a confident, almost predatory grace.

As the transformations completed, the Guardians stood before Venus in their new human forms, each radiating the essence of their true identities. The runes, now etched onto their human skin like intricate tattoos, glowed faintly, a constant reminder of their ancient power.

The atmosphere inside the temple shifted as the Guardians adjusted to their human forms. The beautiful pirate lady, her black hair flowing over her shoulders, let out a sigh of relief.

"I've waited centuries for a drink," she said, a mischievous glint in her eye.

With a wave of her hand, she summoned a silver goblet. She took a long swig of the alcoholic liquid and then belched loudly, the sound echoing through the ancient hall.

The Viking, with his muscular build and braided beard, laughed heartily. "Welcome home, Captain Seraphina!" he said, hitting her on the back with a heavy hand. "I see your spirit hasn't changed one bit."

Seraphina grinned as she stumbled forward, her sharp eyes twinkling with amusement. "And I see you haven't lost your gentle touch, Erik the Bold."

The English gentleman, formerly the Stag, adjusted his top hat and cleared his throat. "Ahem. Allow me to introduce myself properly. I am Sir Reginald, Guardian of the East."

The Roman guard, standing tall and resolute, nodded in acknowledgment. "And I am Marcus Valerius, Guardian of the South. Our purpose here is to protect and to serve."

Erik the Bold, the Viking, thumped his chest with a fist. "Erik the Bold, Guardian of the West. It's good to be back and ready for battle."

Captain Seraphina, the pirate, smirked. "Captain Seraphina, Guardian of the North. Let's make these dark forces regret ever challenging us."

Venus, still in her dog form, listened as each Guardian introduced themselves. The sense of camaraderie and shared purpose was palpable. These were not just powerful beings—they were a united front against the darkness threatening their world.

Sir Reginald, the English gentleman, turned to Venus. "Lady Venus, with your guidance and our combined strength, we will find a way to defeat the Black Magician and restore balance."

Marcus Valerius, the Roman guard, added, "We stand ready to follow your lead, to the very end."

Erik the Bold nodded, his expression fierce and determined. "Together, we will avenge our fallen comrades and protect this world."

Captain Seraphina took another swig from her silver goblet and raised it in a toast. "To victory and to the end of darkness."

"We are ready," said the Bear, his voice now a deep, human baritone. "Thank you, Venus. Together, we will face the Black Magician and restore balance to our world!"

Venus, feeling the weight of her role and the power coursing through her, asked, "What do we do next?"

Evelyn suddenly burst into uncontrollable laughter, her mirth echoing through the ancient temple. The Guardians turned to her, puzzled.

Sir Reginald, the English gentleman, raised an eyebrow. "Pray tell, Miss Evelyn, what is so amusing?"

Through her giggles, Evelyn managed to say, "You... you all look like you're in fancy dress! You can't travel in the world like this. You look ridiculous!"

Captain Seraphina, the pirate, put her hands on her hips and looked at Evelyn with a mock-serious expression. "Ridiculous? I look magnificent!" She took another swig from her silver goblet and let out a hiccup.

Erik the Bold, the Viking, glanced at Sir Reginald and then down at his own attire. "Maybe the lass has a point. We do look a bit conspicuous."

Sir Reginald nodded thoughtfully. "Indeed. What I've seen of the modern world suggests that our current garb might draw undue attention. Lady Venus, might you be able to assist us in adopting more fitting attire?"

Venus, approached the Codex Aetheris once more. The book's pages began to flip, as if guided by an invisible hand, until they settled on the appropriate spell. Venus raised her paw and began to recite the ancient words:

"Vestes temporis mutentur,
Ad mundum hodiernum nos aptentur.
Forma et figura aptentur,
Ut iter nostrum facile fiat."

As the spell's words echoed through the chamber, a soft glow enveloped each of the Guardians. Their elaborate costumes began to shimmer and shift. Sir Reginald's top hat and suit morphed into a smart yet casual outfit—dark jeans, a well-tailored blazer, and a simple button-down shirt.

Erik the Bold's Viking garb transformed into rugged outdoor gear—cargo pants, a flannel shirt, and sturdy army boots. His braided beard remained, giving him a rugged, modern look.

Marcus Valerius's Roman armor melted away, replaced by a leather jacket, dark jeans, and a simple white t-shirt. His stance remained as resolute as ever, but now he looked like he could blend into any crowd.

Captain Seraphina's pirate attire turned into a chic, modern ensemble—a black leather jacket, slim-fitting jeans, and high-heeled boots. Her hair remained wild and untamed, adding to her dramatic presence.

Evelyn clapped her hands in delight. "Much better! Now you all look like you belong in this century."

The Guardians examined their new appearances, nodding in approval. Sir Reginald adjusted his blazer and smiled. "Excellent. Now we can move among the people without drawing undue attention."

Captain Seraphina took another swig from her goblet, which had also transformed into a sleek metal flask. "I'll miss my old outfit, but this will do." She hiccuped again, then laughed.

Venus, satisfied with the results of the transformation spell, returned to her place beside Evelyn. The chamber was now filled with a sense of accomplishment and readiness, yet

Venus could feel the weight of her efforts settling heavily upon her. She lowered herself to the ground, her energy spent but a triumphant gleam still in her only eye.

The Guardians, now attired in modern clothing suitable for blending in with the current world, turned towards Venus. Their expressions conveyed a deep sense of respect and gratitude. Erik the Bold stepped forward, his rugged features softened by a genuine smile.

"Lady Venus," Erik said in a voice that held both reverence and warmth, "you have shown us great kindness and bravery. Without your guidance and magic, we would not have made this transformation. We owe you a debt of gratitude."

Captain Seraphina nodded in agreement, a newfound admiration clear in her eyes. "Aye, you've proven yourself to be more than just a dog with a single eye. You're the key to our mission."

Sir Reginald adjusted his modern attire with a nod of approval. "Indeed, my dear. Your strength and resolve have brought us closer to fulfilling the prophecy."

Marcus Valerius, ever stoic, stepped forward as well. "We are honored to stand by your side, Lady Venus. Your courage will guide us through the challenges ahead."

Venus, though weary, managed a faint but appreciative smile. "Thank you," she murmured, her voice soft yet filled with determination. "But I fear I can go no further in this form. The magic has drained me."

Evelyn, sensing Venus's exhaustion, approached her side and gently placed a hand on her fur. "It's time to rest, Venus," she said softly. "Let Selene take over for now."

With a nod of understanding, Venus closed her eye and concentrated. A shimmering light surrounded her form, swirling and enveloping her until the shape of Selene emerged. Selene, now in her human guise, stood tall and graceful amidst the Guardians.

The Guardians bowed their heads once more, this time in acknowledgment of Selene. She inclined her head in return, her expression one of solemn gratitude. "Thank you, Venus," Selene said, her voice resonating with a quiet strength. "Rest now. We will continue the journey."

Venus, now Selene, stepped back to join Evelyn's side. The Guardians gathered around, their new forms blending seamlessly with the modern world.

Selene then turned her attention to the magical book resting on an ancient stone pedestal. She approached it with an air of reverence, the book hummed softly under her touch, a low resonating vibration that matched the rhythm of her heartbeat.

"With this book," she said, "we will unlock the secrets to defeating our enemy."

Selene raised her hands over the ancient text. Closed her eyes and whispered a chant, a soft incantation that echoed off the walls of the chamber and wrapped around the Guardians like an invisible wave. The room stilled, the air dense with anticipation.

The pages of the book began to flicker, an enchanted wind seeming to breathe life into the inanimate. The sound filled the chamber, each page whispering its own message, its own secret. With a final word from Selene, they stilled. Her fingers slid over the opened passage; her voice rang out clear into the silence as she began to read.

The spell was long and complicated, filled with words of power that echoed through millennia. It spoke of a dark magician whose heart had hardened by time's sands and sorrow. It sang of a hidden location, shrouded in mystery, veiled by deception.

The Guardians listened in silence, their faces etched with determination as Selene's voice took on a rhythm of its own, lilting and strong, filling the chamber with an otherworldly energy. Each word drew out the inherent power of the ancient text, causing the room to tremble with an invisible force. Suddenly, a brilliant light erupted from the book, illuminating each Guardian with a radiant glow. Their forms shone brighter and brighter until they were little more than silhouettes within their vibrant auras.

"By the forces of time and space," Selene chanted, her voice rising above the escalating vibration of energy, "Reveal to us the hidden face!"

As her words echoed within the chamber, the book responded. Pages flickered again as if caught in an unseen gale, faster and faster until they blurred. Then, before the watching eyes of each Guardian, an supernatural image began to form above the open tome. The projection shimmered into existence, appearing much like a mirage born from desert heat; a vision of linear lines shifted and coalesced into the form of the world. It was a fascinating sight, the 3D image rotating gently within the confines of the chamber and casting an unworldly glow on the stone walls.

Mountains, rivers, and oceans passed by as the world spun. Selene continued to chant, her voice now a hushed whisper that barely echoed against the stone walls. Her hands moved gently over the projection, guiding it with an unseen force as she sought the hidden location of their enemy.

Finally, with one final word from Selene, the world stilled. It stopped on a point that shimmered with an icy clarity. The projection zoomed in, revealing an expanse of ice and snow that stretched endlessly into the horizon. The projection illuminated a detail that would have otherwise gone unnoticed - a colossal structure subtly camouflaged by its surroundings.

It was an anomaly, an incongruity amidst the stark white landscape of the Antarctic wilderness. It was a pyramid, its towering silhouette just visible under mounds of snow and ice, its sides gleaming with a strange, icy luminescence. Not Egyptian in design, but older, forgotten by time and mankind. The structure hummed with an ancient power, echoing the resonance of the book from which it had been summoned.

"Beneath the everlasting ice, within the cold heart of winter," Selene whispered, her voice taking on a chilling edge as she recited the final lines of the spell. "Therein lies the hidden lair of our enemy."

The projection grew more detailed, revealing a huge wall of ice encasing one side of the pyramid. The barrier stood tall and strong, glinting dangerously in the Antarctic sunlight. It was clear that this was not a mere construct of nature but a formidable defense infused with potent magic.

"Then we must pierce this frozen fortress," Selene concluded, her eyes gleaming with a determined fire as she gazed at the icy image. "The journey will be perilous, but necessary."

Murmurs of agreement resonated among the Guardians. The image of the snow-entombed pyramid began to fade, its glow dimming until only the haunting echo of its existence remained. The room fell silent once more, save for the rustling of ancient pages returning to their rightful places.

"Now we know where our enemy hides," Selene declared, her voice ringing with a commanding authority that echoed through the chamber. She closed the ancient tome with an air of finality, its leather-bound cover still glowing faintly with residual magic. "Prepare yourselves, Guardians. We must brave the chill of Antarctica and face what lies behind that wall of ice."

The Guardians nodded in understanding, each feeling a surge of adrenaline as they steeled themselves for the impending battle.

"The Ice Pyramid in Antarctica," Selene murmured, her eyes filled with a grim determination.

The structure lay hidden behind a mammoth ice wall, frosty winds howling against its frosty exterior. The image of the pyramid, etched deep within the confines of perennial ice and snow, seemed to have struck a solemn declaration of war into the hearts of everyone present.

"Time is of the essence," Selene's voice echoed, slicing through the apprehensive silence that had fallen over the chamber. Her gaze was firm as she surveyed the room, each Guardian meeting her eyes with a determined nod. "We must act now."

A wave of murmured agreements swept through the room, their collective determination lending the air a tangible weight. Each Guardian radiated an aura of resolve, shimmering golden light reflecting their unity in facing the ominous task ahead.

Selene turned back to the book, her hands hovering over it momentarily before she began to chant again. The words tumbled from her lips in a steady stream, ancient and cryptic as they filled the room with a resonant hum.

As her chant hit its crescendo, the pages of the book once again began to flicker, each one a fluttering blur until they finally came to rest on a new chapter. Her hands traced over the incantations written in an age-old script, as if guiding her through the melody of the ancient spell.

"May the light guide us through the storm," Selene pronounced with a firm voice, the words of the spell echoing around the room like rolling thunder. The aura of each Guardian intensified, their light converging and swirling in a vortex towards the book. An image began to form, a tunnel of light manifesting from the page and extending into the air above them.

On this mystical projection, a glimmering path emerged, winding its way through treacherous ice fields and daunting mountain ranges, towards the hidden pyramid. Each curve and turn carefully marked by symbols and sigils known only to those well-versed in magical arts.

The pathway arrived at the mammoth wall of ice, then coiled upwards over its towering height until it reached the apex of the pyramid's icy crown. The image shimmered and rippled, revealing a single thin line of light that pierced straight into the heart of the ice-bound tomb.

The Guardians stood in awe, their gaze riveted on the intricate display. It was a path filled with danger and uncertainty, but it was their path nonetheless. Their mission was clear: to traverse the treacherous terrains of Antarctica, scale the gigantic ice wall, and infiltrate the frozen sanctuary of their adversary.

The room vibrated with anticipatory tension as Selene closed her chant, her commanding voice fading away to an echo. The magical projection dimmed and collapsed back into the ancient book, leaving behind only a glimmering afterimage.

"May our journey be swift," she spoke softly into the lingering silence. "May our resolve remain unbroken. May our light pierce through darkness. May we return victorious."

A chorus of affirmations followed her solemn words as each Guardian steeled themselves for the journey, their auras pulsating brighter and stronger, as though mirroring the conviction in their hearts. The room resonated with a sense of unity, a shared sense of purpose and resolve, as they prepared to embark on their perilously daunting journey.

Selene felt an electrifying surge of energy coursing through her veins as she stood before her comrades, her heart pounding with the weight of the upcoming ordeal. She glanced at each Guardian, their faces etched with determination and resolute courage. They were ready.

"Let us depart," Selene commanded, her voice resounding confidently, reverberating off the stone walls. "We have a destiny to fulfill."

With that utterance, each Guardian began to glow brighter than before. One by one they stepped forward, their feet treading upon the emblazoned sigils engraved into the ancient stone floor as they moved onto the projected path. Their forms shimmered and flickered momentarily before dissolving into luminous specks of light. This brilliant spectacle was a sight to behold - a dance of stars across the grandeur of an ancient room as each Guardian transformed into a beacon of hope and courage.

Beneath them, the stone sigils pulsed in response, their arcane symbols glowing with power. Evelyn, Beatrice, the wolves and the monkey followed the Guardians, lighting up one after another, like the breadcrumbs in a treacherous forest. The echo of the chant lingered, intertwining with the radiant song of determination that seemed to pulsate from the Guardians.

Selene was the last to step on the sigil-lined path. She cast one final glance at their sanctuary - before stepping onto the projected pathway. Her form shimmered akin to her comrades before dissolving into a brilliant ball of white light.

The room fell into silence once again, now empty of its former occupants but resonating with the lingering energy of their presence. The book lay open on its ancient pedestal, its pages gently rustling in an unseen breeze, the remnants of ancient magic still clinging to its parchment. The world projected from it had disappeared, but the symbols and sigils marking the route to the pyramid continued to smolder with lingering energy.

The silence was profound.

Chapter 8 – 'Silent Unity'

It was as if the winds outside were holding their breath in solidarity with the Guardians and their allies as they embarked on their daunting journey. The elements themselves seemed to whisper words of strength and courage into the night, carrying them all the way to Antarctica, where the icy winds gnashed their teeth against intruders.

Glowing specks of light traveled through windswept snowfields and over chilling ice-covered oceans. They climbed immense snow-laden mountain ranges, shimmered under auroras that painted the sky, and finally navigated through blinding snowstorms, unerringly drawn to the enigmatic pyramid. Each Guardian was a beacon, their light cutting through the dense white canvas of the Antarctic wilderness.

Ice crumbled and whirled in their wake as they pressed onward. The harsh winds seemed to bow under their radiant resolve, parting to create an invisible path. The elements, despite their inherent ferocity, stood bowed in respect, acknowledging the sacredness of their quest.

The monstrous ice wall loomed into sight. The Guardians collided before the grand structure, halting their advance. Seraphina landed hard on her back and rolled in the snow. Their luminous forms shimmered against the frozen landscape. The allies followed and collided with the wall.

The cold, fierce winds of Antarctica roared through the air, its frigid touch seeping into their bones. The Guardians stood proudly in their modern clothing, facing a massive wall of ice that seemed to stretch endlessly towards the sky. It was almost otherworldly, the overwhelming size of the wall making them feel minuscule in comparison to the vast expanse of ice and snow surrounding them.

Bjorn, the Viking Guardian, had morphed into a fearsome bear and stood by the wall's base. With his massive paws and razor-sharp claws, he relentlessly attacked the ice, but the wall stood strong. Despite sending shards of ice flying with each strike, it remained unbreakable, almost taunting them with its invincibility.

"We need another approach," Bjorn growled, frustration evident in his voice as he reverted back to his human form, shaking off the ice from his fur.

Meanwhile, Seraphina, the notorious pirate Guardian, lounged lazily against the ice wall. With a mischievous grin and a glint in her eye, she took slow sips from her silver goblet, likely enjoying the show put on by the bumbling Bjorn. The chill in the air only added to her devilish amusement, while the alcohol brought a rosy glow to her cheeks.

Evelyn turned to her, eyes narrowed. "Seraphina, can you transform and fly up to see how high this wall goes and what's on the other side?"

Seraphina took another long sip, her eyes glassy but alert. She smirked, swaying slightly. "Aye, I can do that, but I can't promise a straight flight. This wall's as tall as a sailor's tale, but I'll give it a go."

The others watched with a mix of anticipation and concern as Seraphina shifted into her eagle form. The transformation was a sight to behold, her form shimmering and twisting until a majestic eagle stood in her place. But as she tried to take off, it was clear that the alcohol had affected her. Her wings beat unevenly, and she wobbled in the air, nearly crashing back down before managing to steady herself.

"Maybe you should lay off the drinks until we're done," Bjorn muttered, but there was a hint of amusement in his voice.

Seraphina, despite her struggles, ascended higher and higher. Her flight was unsteady, but she persevered, her keen eyes scanning the wall as she climbed. The others watched her ascent anxiously, the eagle's form becoming a mere dot against the vast expanse of ice.

Down below, Evelyn voiced the worry on everyone's minds. "Even if we can see over it, how do we get past it? We're trapped here, and even together, we can't fight this many enemies. Look, the trees are bowing under the weight of more troops arriving."

Indeed, the forest at the edge of the ice behind them was filled with dark shapes, the enemy forces massing and pushing forward. They crashed forward in relentless waves.

The sheer number was overwhelming, a tide of hatred and darkness that seemed endless.

Bjorn sighed, looking up at Seraphina's struggling form. "Let's hope she finds something useful up there. We need a miracle to get through this."

As Seraphina climbed higher above the towering ice wall, the biting chill of the Antarctic wind whipped around her. The landscape beneath her became more vivid with altitude, until she crested the top of the wall and gasped at the sight before her before returning to group.

As Seraphina landed gracefully back at the base of the ice wall, she transformed into her human form. Without missing a beat, she immediately reached for her silver goblet and took a deep, hearty swig. Her eyes were wide with the urgency of her discovery, but her hands were steady as she drank.

"What I've seen is extremely dangerous," she said, her voice shaking slightly. "And I need some Dutch courage to get through this." She took another long drink, the liquid within the goblet never seeming to diminish.

The others watched her with a mix of concern and impatience. Evelyn raised an eyebrow. "You really think now is the time to be drinking?"

Seraphina nodded vigorously, her movements a bit unsteady.

"Absolutely. You didn't see what I saw. We're going to need all the courage we can muster." She tipped the goblet back again, draining what seemed to be a considerable amount before letting out a satisfied sigh.

"The goblet is never-ending," she announced with a tipsy grin, her cheeks flushed from the alcohol. "Just what I need for this nightmare."

With that, she took one more large gulp and then collapsed into the snow, the goblet still clutched in her hand.

Bjorn, in his Viking form, stepped forward and looked down at her with a mix of amusement and irritation. "Seraphina, you need to be on your feet, not flat on your back."

He reached down, pulling her up to a sitting position. "Come on, we've got work to do. We need you at the top of your game, not taking an afternoon drunken nap."

Seraphina blinked up at him, her eyes glassy. "I'll be fine. Just give me a moment." She hiccupped, then added, "And you have to admit, I look magnificent."

Bjorn rolled his eyes but couldn't help a small chuckle. "Yes, you do. But save the drinking for after we've dealt with the magician."

As Seraphina tried to steady herself, Evelyn turned to the others. "We're trapped here. Even together, we can't fight this many enemies. Look."

They all turned to see the trees bowing and cracking under the weight of the advancing enemy troops. More black, snarling creatures emerged from the forest, their growling and snapping filling the air.

The Stag, in his human form as Lord Cedric, stepped forward, his eyes dark with worry. "We can't afford to waste time. The longer we stay here, the more enemies will surround us."

Selene spoke calmly. "Seraphina, what have you seen?"

Seraphina, now a bit more coherent, stood up, clutching her goblet. "I've seen what's beyond the wall," she declared, catching her breath. "There's a black stone pyramid covered in glowing runes, and at its top, a crystal that's shooting a laser-like beam of blue energy into the sky. This beam... it's how the magician is controlling the world."

Evelyn and the others listened intently, their faces a mix of awe and concern.

"But that's not all," Seraphina continued, her voice tightening. "Guarding the pyramid is an army of ice golems, dozens of them, perhaps more. They patrol the perimeter in tight, coordinated circles. It's going to be incredibly difficult to get past them."

Bjorn, now in Viking form, gripped his axe with renewed resolve. "We must reach that pyramid, no matter the obstacles. That beam... it must be stopped."

Selene nodded. "We need a smart plan to bypass or disable these golems. We can't delay."

Determined, Seraphina added, "I'll guide us. We'll find a way through the golems and confront the magician."

The frigid winds of Antarctica howled around the group as they gathered at the base of the towering ice wall, the enormity of their task looming as prominently as the structure itself. The atmosphere was tense, filled with the promise of impending conflict as the distant sounds of the advancing hordes echoed across the icy plains.

Beatrice's eyes narrowed against the sharp gusts as she scanned the horizon. The growing cacophony of snarls and stomps signaled the relentless approach of the magician's army, their massive forms glinting menacingly in the sparse sunlight. Each step they took reverberated through the frozen ground, a constant reminder of the impending onslaught.

"We don't have much time," Seraphina said, her voice cutting through the wind with urgency. "They're getting closer. We need to move now."

Bjorn, gripping his axe tightly, nodded in agreement. "The longer we delay, the harder our ascent will be. Those dark creatures won't hesitate to crush us against this wall."

Selene, her fingers brushing against the ice wall, looked up at the daunting height above them. "This barrier isn't just physical—it's a test of our resolve. But remember, we have powers they cannot fathom. We must use every advantage."

As the Guardians gathered at the base of the towering ice wall, a sense of urgency hung in the chilly air. Seraphina, more steady now and focusing on the task at hand, scanned the icy expanse ahead. "Alright, we need to scale this wall. It's the only way to get to the pyramid on the other side."

Bjorn, his Viking form exuding strength and determination, nodded in agreement. "We need to move quickly and quietly. If there's anything out there, they'll be on us if they hear us."

Lord Cedric, transformed into his majestic stag form, looked up at the daunting wall. "I can create a magical pathway up the wall, but it will require all my strength. We need to move fast," he declared, his antlers beginning to glow with a delicate light.

Selene, still feeling the strain from her earlier transformations, stepped forward resolutely. "Let's get started then. We don't have any time to waste."

Lord Cedric closed his eyes, concentrating deeply. Ancient runes began to form along the ice wall, creating a shimmering pathway that spiraled upwards. The runes cast an eerie glow on the ice, illuminating their path.

"Go!" Lord Cedric commanded; his voice filled with urgency. The group quickly started their ascent, with Evelyn and Beatrice leading, followed by Selene, Bjorn, and finally Seraphina, who clutched her goblet tightly. Finally, the wolves followed closely behind, the monkey clinging to the Alpha wolf's back.

The group, accompanied by their loyal wolf companions, ascended the enchanted pathway carved into the icy wall. The Alpha wolf, ever vigilant, kept a keen eye on the approaching army below while leading the pack with deft and surefooted steps. Their urgency was clear in the sound of their paws against the frozen surface. As they climbed higher, the ruins beneath them crumbled and faded away, leaving no possibility for retreat. With every step upwards, the consequences of slipping grew greater; one wrong move would result in certain death.

"Quickly now, but watch your step!" the Alpha called back to the pack, his voice firm and commanding. The wolves moved with a mix of haste and caution, their natural agility tested by the slick, treacherous surface of the wall.

The thunderous roars of the shadowy army reverberated against the towering wall below, assaulting the senses with a relentless onslaught of noise and chaos. The unyielding forces relentlessly slammed into the barrier in an unending wave, their high-pitched shrieks and howls hauntingly echoing up to the group above. With each impact, the ground trembled with fear, a constant reminder of the peril lurking below. The colossal, dark figures and clawed hands of the enemy ceaselessly pounded at the ice, causing violent vibrations along the wall, but Lord Cedric's potent magic flickered fiercely, holding steady and keeping the runes blazing with defensive power.

The final wolf in the pack, a young but determined member, skidded on an icy patch. His paws scrabbled against the frozen surface as he frantically tried to regain his balance.

The Alpha wolf's voice rang out, filled with both urgency and care. "Steady there!" he called out. "Keep your focus. We're almost there."

Encouraged by their leader's voice, the young wolf adjusted his approach. With a determined push, he regained his pace, moving swiftly to catch up with the rest of the pack.

As the final wolf crested the top of the wall, he let out a soft whine of relief, quickly stifled as he joined the others in formation. The last of the glowing runes faded behind them, the magical pathway disappearing. The wall returned to its sheer, smooth state, an insurmountable barrier to the unmagical.

The Alpha wolf surveyed his pack, ensuring all were accounted for and unharmed. "Well done, everyone," he praised, his tone allowing a momentary breath of relief before he turned his attention forward. "But keep alert. We must support the Guardians and prepare for what lies ahead at the pyramid."

As the Guardians gathered at the summit of the ice wall, taking in the sight of the ice golems amassing below, a momentary silence fell over the group. The urgency of their situation was obvious, and each of them felt the weight of their task.

Evelyn, wrapping her cloak tighter against the cold, looked to Selene, "Selene, do you know of anything that might help us handle those golems if they decide to follow or block our path to the pyramid?"

Selene thought for a moment before responding, "There may be a few spells that could temporarily hinder them, but nothing long-lasting. We'll have to think outside the box and act fast."

Lord Cedric, now in his human form, straightened his coat and weighed their options. "Our only hope is to use our stealth and agility. We cannot win in a direct confrontation against such a massive army, but we can outwit them."

Seraphina, back in her human form and still clutching her goblet, chimed in with a smirk, "And if anyone can sneak past a bunch of oversized ice sculptures, it's us. I did see a few gaps in their patrols from above. We could exploit those."

Bjorn nodded, his expression grim but determined. "Then that's our path. We exploit every weakness, every gap. No direct confrontations unless absolutely necessary."

Marcus Valerius, who had been quietly assessing the situation, spoke up. "And while we move, we must keep an eye on that beam. It's not just a weapon; it's a tether holding whatever dark power the magician is channeling. Severing that might be key to defeating him."

Evelyn turned to the group, her leadership clear. "Alright, we stick together, move fast, and keep to the shadows. Use the environment to our advantage, and keep communication open. We cannot afford any mistakes—not here, not now."

As the group nodded in agreement, Seraphina took to the skies once more, her eagle eyes scouting the path ahead.

Chapter 9 – 'An Ingenious Descent'

In the shadow of the towering ice wall, Marcus Valerius, the Roman Soldier Guardian of the South, stepped forward with a strategic idea born from his ancient Roman engineering knowledge. The icy descent posed a formidable challenge, and Marcus knew they needed a method that was both rapid and secure.

"Friends," Marcus began, his voice resonating with the gravitas of his centuries of experience, "in ancient Rome, we engineered roads and bridges to conquer impossible terrains. Here, we must engineer our descent."

He turned to Selene. "Do you know of any spell that can temporarily manipulate ice? If so, I could use it to create a controlled slide, much like a frozen aqueduct, to safely bring us to the ground."

Selene nodded thoughtfully. "Yes, there is a spell called *'Viam Glaciae Descensus'.* It can soften and shape the ice for a short time. Does that sound familiar?"

Marcus's face lit up with recognition. "Indeed! I recall studying its applications."

Selene gestured for him to proceed. "Please, continue."

Encouraged, Marcus stepped forward with confidence. He raised his arms, palms facing the icy expanse, and began to chant the spell with a commanding voice:

"Viam Glaciae Descensus!
Cursum naturae ad meum voco,
Glaciem formate ad descensum placidum,
Ut via nostra sit secura et celer."

As he chanted, the air around his hands shimmered with a cold blue energy that seeped into the ice wall. The surface began to ripple and flow like water, gradually reshaping itself into a smooth, wide chute that spiraled down the ice wall, gleaming under the dim Antarctic light.

Satisfied with his work, Marcus turned to his companions, who watched in awe. "The Via Glacia has been formed. We can now descend swiftly and safely. Let us proceed with caution and haste."

One by one, the Guardians approached the newly formed ice chute. Captain Seraphina, her bravery evident, was the first to test the path. She slid down with a laugh, followed by the others, who experienced the thrill of the descent while marveling at Marcus's skillful use of ancient magic.

At the base of the ice wall, an uneasy calm settled over the snowy expanse. This tranquility was abruptly shattered as the ground beneath the pristine snow began to rumble ominously. Ice golems, intricately carved with ancient magical runes, began to rise from the glacier around the pyramid. The ice cracked and groaned as these colossal figures emerged, their synchronized movements forming a protective circle around the pyramid. Their deliberate placement suggested a strategic defensive formation.

Selene observed the golems and quickly grasped the complexity of their challenge. "These golems are positioned to cover each other's weaknesses. We need a plan that outsmarts their formation," she said, scanning the battlefield for potential gaps.

Lord Cedric, in his stag form, nodded in agreement. "Their arrangement creates a nearly impenetrable barrier around the pyramid. We may need to divide and conquer, targeting smaller groups to break their defense."

Bjorn clenched his fists. "I can engage a few head-on to test their reaction speed and strength. It will give us an idea of their combat capabilities."

Before they could clash with the ice golems, Selene gathered Evelyn and Beatrice for an important discussion. The stark white backdrop of the Antarctic landscape underscored the gravity of her words.

"You both are crucial to our success," Selene began, her tone serious. "There is a spell, Warrior's Ascendancy, that can transform you into formidable warriors, enhancing both your physical combat abilities and magical prowess."

Evelyn and Beatrice listened intently, recognizing the gravity of the decision before them.

"However," Selene continued, her gaze steady, "this transformation is not without risks. The spell will push your mortal bodies to their limits, enhancing your strength, speed, and agility, but it will also strain you physically and mentally. You will be more vulnerable to attack because your senses will be heightened to an almost unbearable degree."

Selene paused to ensure her next words were clear. "While transformed, you remain mortal. Any injury you sustain could be severe or worse. I need to know you're fully aware of these dangers and still willing to proceed. I will only cast this spell if you're certain."

Evelyn and Beatrice exchanged a glance, their resolve solidifying. After a moment of silent communication, they turned back to Selene, their expressions determined.

"We understand the risks," Evelyn said firmly. "We're ready. The power you're offering could turn the tide of this battle. We trust you and ourselves to handle these new powers."

Beatrice nodded. "We're sure, Selene. This risk is necessary for the mission. We need every advantage, and if this spell provides that edge, we accept the consequences."

Selene regarded them with a mix of pride and concern. "Very well. I will perform the incantation. Remember to stay aware of your limits and look out for each other."

Selene closed her eyes, summoning her magical knowledge, and raised her hands toward Evelyn and Beatrice. Her voice, resonant and clear, echoed against the icy backdrop:

"Audite me, o potestates terrae,
Mutatio essentiae,
revelate fortitudinem occulta!
Corpus et animus,
accipite vigorem et agilitatem,
Transformati ex voluntate mea,
ad bellum parati!"

As she chanted, a subtle glow enveloped Evelyn and Beatrice, forming a shimmering aura. The incantation, rooted in ancient Latin, tapped into their hidden strengths:

"Hear me, powers of the earth,
Change their essence, reveal hidden strength!
Body and mind, receive vigor and agility,
Transformed by my will, ready for battle!"

The glow intensified, casting a brilliant golden light. Evelyn and Beatrice felt a surge of energy awakening every cell, sharpening their senses, and invigorating their bodies. They stood taller, their eyes reflecting newfound capabilities, ready to confront the formidable ice golems.

"Remember," Selene cautioned as the transformation settled, "these powers are potent but taxing. Use them wisely and maintain your sense of self amidst the battle."

Evelyn and Beatrice nodded, feeling the raw power coursing through them. Beatrice flexed her hands, amazed at the energy and strength she felt. Evelyn tested her enhanced reflexes, her movements swift and precise.

"Wow," Beatrice murmured, "I've never felt anything like this."

Evelyn, grinning with newfound confidence, said, "Let's hope this lasts long enough to make a difference. Thank you, Selene."

Selene, recognizing the need for specialized weaponry to complement their new abilities, began an ancient spell to conjure mythical weapons. Her voice, steady and commanding, echoed across the icy landscape:

"Arma antiqua,

Venite ad me,

Ex nihilo,

Aetheris filum,

Formate figuras,

Fortitudinis symbola!"

As she chanted, the air shimmered with a silver light. For Evelyn, the particles coalesced into a sleek, elegant sword, its blade resembling frozen light, edged with glowing runes. The hilt was wrapped in white leather with a crystalline wolf pommel, symbolizing her leadership and cunning.

Beatrice's weapon materialized as twin daggers, curved like the crescent moon. Lighter than they appeared, they were perfect for her agility, etched with symbols of protection and swiftness, their hilts adorned with sparkling sapphires. Along with these, they received bows and quivers filled with enchanted arrows, crafted to enhance accuracy and range.

With the weapons now in hand, Selene completed the spell with a binding incantation. *"Vinculum!"* A pulse of energy surged, binding the weapons to Evelyn and Beatrice physically and spiritually.

"Use these with honor and bravery," Selene advised. "They are more than mere tools; they are partners in the battles to come."

Evelyn and Beatrice tested their new weapons, feeling their natural fit. As they prepared, the distant rumbling of advancing golems broke the calm.

"We don't have much time," Selene warned. "These weapons will serve you well, but we must rejoin the others and prepare for the fight."

Evelyn gripped her sword tightly. "Let's make haste. With these in hand, I'm ready to face whatever comes."

Beatrice, twirling her daggers, added, "Yes, every moment we delay gives the golems a stronger position. We must act swiftly."

Selene gathered the group, signaling to Bjorn, Lord Cedric, and the others forming a defensive perimeter. "The golems are nearly upon us. Evelyn and Beatrice are now fully prepared. Let's use their enhanced abilities to our advantage."

Bjorn nodded in approval. "Good, we need every edge. Evelyn, take the left flank with Beatrice. Your agility and new weapons will be crucial in breaking their ranks."

As the battle loomed, the Guardians braced themselves for the fight, knowing that their preparation and unity would be tested against the formidable ice golems.

Chapter 10 – 'Frozen Fury'

The Antarctic winds howled around the Guardians as they braced for the inevitable clash. The ice golems, towering figures of ancient frost and magic, marched relentlessly towards them, their massive forms reflecting the dim light with a menacing gleam. As the first golem reached the group, the battle erupted with ferocity.

Bjorn, with a roaring battle cry, met the first golem head-on. His axe swung with tremendous force, chipping away large chunks of ice from the golem's body. Yet, for every piece he shattered, the golem seemed to regenerate, the ancient runes on its body glowing brighter, pulling moisture from the air to reform its icy shell.

Evelyn and Beatrice, utilizing their new warrior abilities, moved swiftly on the flank. Evelyn's sword glowed with a fierce light, slicing through ice with precision, while Beatrice's daggers whirled in deadly arcs, targeting the joints and weaker points Seraphina's eagle eyes identified from above. Despite their enhanced prowess, the golems' sheer numbers and regenerative abilities made each victory short-lived, as fallen shards reformed into new adversaries.

Lord Cedric and Marcus, now in his giant wolf form, stood shoulder to shoulder in the center, using their combined strength to create a defensive bulwark. Lord Cedric's antlers radiated a magical barrier that deflected some of the golems' blows, while the Wolf's brute force was essential in keeping the golems at bay. However, the relentless assault began to wear down their defenses, the constant barrage testing the limits of their magical endurance.

Seraphina, from her vantage point in the sky, directed the Guardians to concentrate their efforts on a particularly large golem that was coordinating the attack. She dove, her talons aimed at the golem's rune-covered head, but a swift, icy blast knocked her from her trajectory, sending her tumbling to the snow below.

As Seraphina struggled to regain her bearings on the ground, Selene realized the tide was turning against them, as she watched the battle like an ancient commander at war.

As the battle wore on, fatigue and the sheer force of the golems began to overwhelm the Guardians. Evelyn and Beatrice found themselves back-to-back, surrounded by reforming ice warriors.

Bjorn, nearby, was slowed by a deep gash across his arm where an ice shard had struck him, his movements becoming labored.

Lord Cedric, seeing the dire situation, made a call for retreat to a more defensible position. "Regroup!" he bellowed, his voice cutting through the clamor of the battle. "We need a new strategy!"

The Guardians, supporting each other, began a tactical withdrawal, moving towards a narrow ice canyon that would limit the golems' ability to surround them. As they retreated, the realization that they were not just fighting ice but a cunning, magical intelligence became clearer. The golems didn't merely attack; they herded and anticipated, adapting to every move the Guardians made.

As they reached the safety of the canyon's mouth, the Guardians took a moment to catch their breath, assess their injuries, and prepare for the next phase of their desperate struggle. The fight was far from over, and they needed to quickly devise a plan that could exploit the golems' weaknesses more effectively if they were to survive and reach the pyramid.

As the Guardians quickly regrouped in the narrow ice canyon, their breaths visible in the frigid air, they huddled for a brief strategy session. The sheer canyon walls provided a natural choke point, a strategic advantage they needed to exploit to fend off the golem assault.

Bjorn, his arm bloodied but his spirit undeterred, wiped his axe on his cloak and addressed the group with authority. "We've been too spread out," he grunted. "Here in this canyon, we can control their numbers, face them one wave at a time. Evelyn, Beatrice, your strength of heart has been key. Keep focusing on their vulnerabilities."

Evelyn nodded, tightening her grip on her newly enchanted sword, and Beatrice reassured him, "We'll keep fighting. Just tell us where to hit them hardest."

Lord Cedric, always the tactician, pointed towards the narrowest part of the canyon. "We hold them here. I'll reinforce this point with a barrier. Selene, can you boost the barrier's strength?"

Selene, her hands already glowing with preparatory magic, responded, "I'm on it. We'll make this pass a freezing hell for them."

Seraphina, now back in her human form, checked her bow before responding. "I'll take the high ground, cover you from above. If they break through, I'll see it first."

Selene felt her agility would be less effective in the cramped space but knew Venus in her dog form could still contribute significantly. She reached out to Venus telepathically within her own mind, "It's time for you to join the battle," she communicated firmly. "You might be small now, but you can still create chaos. If you nip at their heels, keep them turned around, you can really make a difference." With that Selene transformed in Venus, who stood now assessing the situation.

As the first of the ice golems entered the canyon, Bjorn and Lord Cedric stood at the forefront. Cedric's staff glowed as he chanted, strengthening the icy barrier that spanned across the canyon mouth. Bjorn roared as he met the lead golem with a powerful swing of his axe, the impact echoing like thunder.

"Focus on the joints, Beatrice! That's their weak spot!" Evelyn called out as she parried a blow from another golem, her blade slicing through its arm.

Beatrice, drawing her bow with precision, directed an arrow at a golem's knee, as instructed. The arrow struck true, causing the golem to stumble as cracks spread from the impact.

"Good call, Evelyn!" Beatrice shouted over the din of battle, nocking another arrow and taking aim.

Seraphina, perched above, let an arrow fly, finding its mark in the eye of an approaching golem. "Keep it up! They're slowing down!" she yelled, drawing another arrow.

The battle grew fierce as more golems pushed into the canyon. The Guardians, now unified in their strategy, worked seamlessly. Bjorn and Cedric's frontline defense, combined with Evelyn and Beatrice's tactical arrow-based assaults and Seraphina's precise covering attacks, gradually turned the tide in their favor.

"Stay sharp! They're not stopping yet!" Bjorn shouted as he cleaved through another golem. "Evelyn, Beatrice, keep hitting them hard!"

Venus now joined the others in battle and darted around the battlefield, her small form zipped through the golems' legs, biting and dodging. Her attacks, although minor, distracted the golems enough for the others to exploit their brief moments of confusion.

Their coordinated defense held strong, each Guardian playing their part flawlessly. The ice canyon, once just a geographical feature, had become the linchpin in their battle strategy, showcasing the power of their unity and resolve under Bjorn's leadership.

As the Guardians regrouped in the ice canyon, Seraphina, in eagle form, having studied various arcane constructs, swooped down and shared a crucial piece of knowledge she recalled from an ancient tome. "These golems," she explained, glancing at the approaching figures, "are powered by a blue heartstone embedded within their cores. It's the source of their animation and regeneration capabilities. If we can shatter these heartstones, the golems will lose their power and crumble."

Bjorn nodded, quickly formulating a plan. "Alright, we focus on exposing their cores. Evelyn, Beatrice, your arrow-based attacks could be perfect for this. Aim for their chests, try to crack open a path to these heartstones."

Evelyn and Beatrice adjusted their positions, readying their arrows specifically designed to target and weaken the icy armor protecting the golems' central cores.

As the next wave of golems advanced into the canyon, the Guardians put their plan into action. Seraphina, from her vantage point above, identified the lead golem whose heartstone faintly glowed through its translucent chest. She signaled to the group, diving down to distract the creature by raking her talons across its eyes, drawing its attention upward.

Taking advantage of the distraction, Bjorn charged forward, his axe swinging with a mighty roar, creating deep gashes in the golem's icy exterior. Evelyn followed up with a precise shot from her bow, the arrow imbued with a piercing spell designed to target the golem's heartstone. The arrow struck true, shattering the ice and exposing the shimmering blue heartstone within. The impact sends cracks spider-webbing through it, and with a resonant crack, the heartstone shatters.

The golem stumbles, its movements becoming erratic as the light from its heartstone dims. With a final groan, it collapses into a pile of inert ice shards, no longer animated by the magical energy of the heartstone.

Encouraged by their success, the Guardians repeat this tactic. Lord Cedric transforms into the Stag and stands with Marcus transformed into the giant Wolf, coordinating to keep the golems at bay, using defensive spells and physical barriers, while Seraphina continues to provide aerial support, pinpointing the golems whose heartstones are most accessible.

As they pause momentarily to catch their breath, Lord Cedric assesses their progress and suggests an adjustment. "Let's keep them funneled into this narrow pass. It limits how many can come at us at once. Venus and the wolves, can you run interference? Lead them straight into our traps."

Selene, in her form as Venus, nods and dashes forward, her smaller size and agility perfect for weaving through the golem's ranks, drawing them into the Guardians' prepared ambushes.

This approach adds tactical depth to your battle scenes, combining direct combat with strategic exploitation of the golem's specific vulnerability. The Guardians now have the ability to adapt and utilize their unique skills in synergy to start to overcome the formidable enemy that confronts them.

As Bjorn charged into the fray with a thunderous roar, his powerful axe struck the first golem, tearing large chunks of ice from its formidable body. Despite the force of his blows, the golem's body began to shimmer and heal itself, runes glowing ominously as they absorbed moisture from the surrounding air, reforming the ice almost as quickly as it was destroyed.

"Persistent beasts, aren't they?" Bjorn grunted, swinging his axe again with determined force. "But we've got more tricks up our sleeves!"

To his side, Evelyn and Beatrice leveraged their enhanced abilities, swiftly maneuvering to the golems' flanks. Evelyn's sword, infused with a magical glow, cut through the ice with enhanced precision, leaving glowing trails in the air with each slice. Beatrice, with agility heightened by the spell, danced around the golems, her daggers slicing through the air, targeting vulnerabilities that Seraphina called out from her aerial vantage point.

"Evelyn, aim for the chest! There's a weak spot just below the shoulder joint!" Seraphina shouted from above, diving and swooping to distract another golem.

"Got it!" Evelyn replied, adjusting her stance and driving her sword deep into the indicated spot. The blade met resistance and then slid through, finding the gap in the icy armor.

Beside her, Beatrice followed up, "Cover me!" she called out, as she darted in. Her daggers struck precisely, exploiting the opening Evelyn had created, aiming to deepen the wound and prevent the golem from regenerating.

Despite their concerted efforts and the enhancements they wielded, the sheer number of golems and their relentless ability to regenerate made the battle increasingly desperate. The shards of ice that Bjorn and the others knocked loose seemed to have a life of their own, crawling and merging to form new golem figures.

"We need to focus our attacks," Beatrice suggested, panting from exertion. "Target their cores; it's the only way to put them down for good!"

Bjorn nodded in agreement, catching his breath. "Seraphina, keep those eyes sharp. We need to know where to hit them hardest."

"Understood!" Seraphina called back, her voice echoing as she circled above, her sharp eyes scanning for the glowing heartstones within the golems.

As they regrouped for another coordinated strike, the Guardians felt the weight of the battle pressing in. Yet, their resolve did not waver, each member ready to adapt and overcome, knowing that their combined strength and strategy were key to breaking through the icy ranks of their formidable foes.

As the battle against the ice golems raged fiercely around the canyon, Seraphina, the Eagle Guardian, soared high above the chaos. Her sharp eyes caught a glimpse of something unusual on the exterior of the pyramid — a series of air vents or grids that could possibly serve as an entry point.

"Slight change of plan!" Seraphina shouted down to the group, her voice piercing through the din of battle. "There are vents on the pyramid that might be small enough for Venus and the monkey to sneak through!"

Marcus Valerius, the Giant Wolf Guardian, who had been ferociously battling a particularly large golem, turned towards her voice. With a swift, powerful movement, he delivered a crushing blow with his clawed paw, that shattered the golem's heartstone, causing the construct to crumble into a pile of ice shards. "Lead the way, Seraphina! We'll cover their advance!"

With the plan quickly set, Marcus rallied the wolves, including the Alpha. "We need to clear a path and buy them some time. Focus on confusion and disruption. Keep the golems off balance!"

The wolves, understanding their role, intensified their attacks, darting in and out of the golem ranks with strategic precision. The Alpha wolf, with a deep, resonating howl, led a charge that drew several golems away from the path to the pyramid.

Meanwhile, Venus, in her swift dog form, and the monkey, always ready for mischief, prepared to make their dash to the vents. The monkey, despite the seriousness of their mission, couldn't resist performing a quick somersault, eliciting a brief, amused snort from Venus before she nudged him towards their goal with her nose.

"Stay close to me," Venus barked softly to the monkey, who nodded and tightened his grip on a small blade he'd pilfered from one of the Guardian's belts — a potential key to unlocking the grates.

As they sprinted towards the pyramid, Seraphina dove towards the vents, her talons outstretched. With precise, powerful jerks, she ripped off the grates, clearing the way for Venus and the monkey. "Go now!" she screeched, keeping an eye on the approaching golems who had noticed the disturbance.

Venus and the monkey quickly slipped through the opening, disappearing into the dark interior of the pyramid just as Marcus and the Alpha wolf arrived at the scene to fend off the golems attempting to follow.

Marcus, with a warrior's cry, engaged another golem, his massive paws and sharp instincts allowing him to maneuver around its attacks and find its heartstone. With a forceful swipe, he smashed the stone, sending another enemy into a cascade of ice and snow.

The battle continued. Evelyn, Beatrice, and Bjorn, supported by Lord Cedric's magical barriers, kept the remaining golems engaged, using every ounce of their enhanced abilities and tactical knowledge to hold the line.

Chapter 11 – 'Digital Menace'

As Venus and Chico, the monkey ventured deeper into the dark corridors of the pyramid, a cold, artificial light began to flicker on from the walls around them. The corridors were lined with digital screens that suddenly illuminated, revealing the sinister visage of the magician. His image flickered across multiple displays, his expression one of contemptuous amusement.

"Ah, Selene, I knew you would return, hiding within a dog, I see. You are now a coward before me." His voice echoed through the corridors, chilling despite the digital distortion. "You and your little band of Guardians think you can thwart me, but you are merely players on a stage I have designed. My consciousness lives within the net, beyond your reach. I am immortal, omnipresent."

Venus, feeling the weight of their mission, listened intently. Inside her mind, Selene's voice offered guidance and reassurance. "Remember, Venus, we're here for a purpose. Don't let him distract you. We need to reach the power core."

The monkey clung to Venus, his eyes wide with fear as the magician's monologue continued. "The leaders of your world are under my influence. I control them through the vast web I have woven. Your efforts here are futile. And now, the world watches you, live, as you attempt to dismantle their savior."

As they progressed down the endless corridors and turns of the pyramid's interior, Selene noticed it all seemed familiar to her, remembering her past encounters with the magician. Telepathically she spoke to Venus directly. "This layout, it's like his old castle. I believe the power core, the heart of his operation, is at the center. That's where we must go."

The walls beside them transitioned from digital screens to massive glass panels, behind which rows upon rows of humming data banks descended into the depths of the pyramid. The glow from these panels cast eerie shadows, but provided just enough light to navigate the labyrinthine interior.

Venus, keeping the monkey close, whispered encouragingly, "Stay with me, we need each other to get through this."

Navigating through the digital maze, they followed Selene's mental instructions, which were based on her memories of the magician's castle. Each turn and doorway brought them closer to the heart of the pyramid.

As they approached the central chamber, the magician's voice boomed once more through the space, echoing off the cold, hard surfaces. "You are too late, Selene. The world is mine to command. They see you as invaders, as threats to their peace. How long before they turn against you?"

Selene's telepathic voice in Venus's mind was calm and focused. "Don't listen to him. He wants to sow doubt and fear. Remember, we only need to reach the core. Disable it, and his control over the networks will falter."

Emerging into the central chamber, they were confronted with a massive structure resembling a core, pulsating with light and energy. The screens around them displayed the live feed of their own progress, watched by millions.

Determined, Venus readied herself for whatever came next, her resolve bolstered by Selene's guidance and the urgent need to end the magician's reign. The final confrontation loomed, promising a clash of wills and technology that would determine the fate of the world.

As Venus and the monkey approached the pulsating power core at the center of the pyramid, more screens around them flickered to life. The magician's visage reappeared; his eyes gleaming with malevolent triumph.

"You fools," he began, his voice reverberating through the chamber, "you think you can disrupt my reign? I have already contacted the world's forces and the social media giants. They have begun a propaganda war against you, painting you as the true enemies of peace and order."

The magician gestured dramatically, and the screens shifted to show news broadcasts and social media feeds. Headlines and posts depicted the Guardians as terrorists and threats to global stability.

"The government air force has been infiltrated via their phones and computers," he continued, his voice dripping with contempt, "and a mobile air force is already in the air. Soon, the skies will rain destruction upon you."

On some of the screens, live footage showed fighter jets taking off, their engines roaring as they launched with full payloads. The magician's voice grew even more arrogant. "I am more powerful than you can imagine. The world is now my slave, and they will protect me at all costs. I have given them knowledge and power, and in return, they are my subjects to command."

Venus felt a pang of fear but quickly shook it off, listening to Selene's calm, steadying voice in her mind. "Don't let him intimidate you, Venus. His power relies on fear and manipulation. Focus on our mission."

Venus looked at the monkey, who was visibly trembling. "Hey, stay with me," she said softly. "We need to finish this. Remember, we're not just doing this for us but for everyone out there."

The monkey nodded, clutching his dagger tightly as they moved closer to the core. The path was illuminated by the eerie glow of the digital screens, showing a world under siege by the magician's influence.

The power core stood before them, a massive structure pulsating with energy. The screens around them continued to show the chaos outside, but Venus and the monkey were undeterred.

"Here it is," Selene's voice echoed in Venus's mind. "We disrupt this, and his control over the networks will falter. It's now or never."

As Venus and the monkey approached the core, the magician's face reappeared on the screens, his expression twisted with rage. "You are too late!" he bellowed. "The world is mine to command, and soon, you will be nothing but a memory."

As Venus and the monkey stood before the pulsating power core, the screens surrounding them flickered, showing the dire situation outside. The Guardians were being forced back, the ice golems regenerating faster than they could be destroyed. The wolves were thrown through the air by the powerful blows of the golems. The battle was turning against them.

Inside Venus's mind, Selene's voice was calm but filled with a deep, ancient sorrow. "Venus, the time has come," she began. "I have lived a thousand lives and fought many battles. I am tired. I have faced this magician before, and last time, it cost me and the Guardians dearly. We lost everything we held dear."

Venus's resolve strengthened with Selene's words, though she could feel the weight of her mentor's weariness. "But we can't lose now, Selene," Venus thought back. "We've come too far."

The screens switched to the pilots in the planes, receiving orders. "Coordinates are set. Use all necessary force to destroy the site of the pyramid," the orders commanded. The lead pilot, flying in formation, spoke over the radio, "Two minutes to destination. Payload is loaded and hot."

The magician's laughter echoed through the chamber, a chilling sound that reverberated through Venus and the monkey. "You see," he sneered, "I am prepared. You think this is my only stronghold? This is a trap, a death trap for the Guardians. This time you will be destroyed and never return."

The screens showed the fighter jets closing in on their target, their payloads ready to unleash destruction. Venus felt a surge of fear but quickly focused on Selene's voice.

"Venus, you must understand," Selene continued, her tone both urgent and gentle. "This is our last chance. I have lost to him before. But this time, we have something we didn't have before: you. You can succeed where I failed."

Venus, sensing the gravity of the situation, looked at the monkey, who was trembling with fear. "Stay close, we can do this," she reassured him softly. "We have to."

With renewed determination, Venus approached the power core. The screens around them continued to show the chaotic battle outside, the Guardians struggling to hold their ground. The golems were relentless, their regeneration seemingly unstoppable.

"Selene, tell me what to do," Venus thought, her mind focused on the task at hand.

"You must disrupt the power core," Selene instructed. "Find the central conduit and sever it. It will destabilize the entire structure and break his control. But be careful, Venus. The core is heavily protected. You'll need to work quickly."

Venus nodded, feeling the surge of adrenaline. "Let's do this," she whispered, more to herself than to the monkey, who clung to her side, ready to assist however he could.

As they neared the core, the magician's image appeared again, his eyes blazing with fury. "You are too late!" he bellowed. "The world is mine to command, and you are nothing but pawns in my grand design. This ends now!"

Ignoring his taunts, Venus focused on the glowing heart of the power core. The monkey, overcoming his fear, climbed onto the structure and began to look for weak points, using the small dagger he had carried with him to stab randomly at the control panel.

With Selene's guidance, Venus identified the central conduit. "Here it is," she thought. "This is where we strike."

Together, Venus and the monkey began to sever the conduit, their efforts a blend of determination and desperation. The core resisted, its defenses impenetrable to Venus's bites and the monkey's blade, but they pressed on, driven by the knowledge that their success was the only hope for the Guardians and the world.

As the lead pilot's voice echoed from the screens, "One minute to destination," Venus knew they were racing against time. Every second counted. The magician's trap was closing, but they were determined to turn it into their victory.

The final showdown had begun, and the fate of the world hung in the balance.

As Venus and the monkey continued to work on severing the central conduit, Selene's voice in Venus's mind became more urgent. "Venus, there's something I need to tell you. The only way to truly destroy the magician is for me to enter the network myself. From within, I can disrupt his control and turn his power for good."

Venus's heart sank at the realization. "But how, Selene? How can you enter the network?"

"The necklace," Selene explained. "You need to take off the necklace and throw it into the power source orb. It's the only way to transfer my essence into the network. Once there, I can dismantle his control from the inside."

Venus shook her head, tears welling up in her eye. "I can't do that, Selene. I won't risk your life. There has to be another way."

Selene's voice was calm and resolute. "Venus, this is the only way. This was foretold in the prophecy, a part only the Guardians and I knew about. One must lay down their life to save all. I am prepared for this."

Venus's heart ached with the weight of the decision. "I can't. I won't. I need you, Selene."

"It's okay, Venus," Selene reassured her. "You've grown so much. You're strong enough to lead the Guardians. Trust me, this is what must be done."

Venus, unable to bring herself to remove the necklace, turned to the monkey, her eyes pleading. "I can't do it, but you can. Please, do it for me."

The monkey, his eyes sad but understanding, grunted softly and nodded. He reached up and caught the enchanted necklace, as it magically released itself from the neck of Venus and fell. Holding it carefully, he looked at Venus one last time before turning to the orb.

The magician's image flickered on the screens, his voice full of rage and desperation. "What are you doing? You think this will stop me? I will not be defeated by a simple creature and a dog!"

The monkey, undeterred by the magician's threats, threw the necklace into the power source orb. The orb began to glow with an intense, blinding light, and the room filled with a resonant hum as Selene's essence merged with the network.

The magician's voice grew frantic. "No! You cannot do this! I am eternal! I am invincible!"

But it was too late. The power core surged, and the screens around them flickered with chaotic images as Selene began to disrupt the magician's control. The magical energy within the pyramid pulsed wildly, and the structure itself seemed to shudder.

Outside, the Guardians saw the effects immediately. The golems began to falter, their regenerative abilities weakening. The fighter jets, now closing in on their target, started to veer off course as their systems were compromised.

Venus felt Selene's presence fading but also sensed a new strength within herself. "Thank you, Selene," she whispered. "We'll finish this for you."

The magician's image flickered one last time, his expression one of pure fury. "You will pay for this! The world will never forgive you!"

As Venus and the monkey watched the power core surge with energy, the screens around them flickered and then suddenly displayed an image of Selene. She seemed to be fighting a shadowy figure, her movements quick and desperate. Turning towards Venus, she shouted, her voice filled with urgency and fear, "Run! Get out of here now! Use telepathy to communicate with the monkey!"

The building began to shake violently, and digital screens around them started to smoke and explode. Venus and the monkey shared a brief, terrified glance. "We have to go, now!" Venus thought desperately, using her telepathic link with the monkey. "If we don't get out of here, this place is going to explode!"

The monkey screamed, waving his hands frantically as he took off running, Venus close on his heels. They sprinted through the corridors, the digital walls around them bursting into flames and debris. As they passed the massive databanks which now sparked and burst into flame, Venus stole a quick glance through a window and saw the fire rising towards them, the sheer scale of the chaos within the pyramid was now unstoppable.

"I don't know if we'll make it," Venus communicated telepathically, her heart pounding in her chest, "but we have to try!"

The orb in the center of the pyramid finally succumbed to the overwhelming surge of energy and exploded. Outside, the Guardians, still locked in combat with the golems, suddenly stopped as they witnessed a massive pulse of violet light shoot up into the sky from the pyramid's apex. The force of the explosion rocked the ground, and a plume of smoke and ash began to rise, filling the air with a dark cloud.

The golems, cut off from their power source, ceased their movements and shattered into countless pieces. Evelyn, seeing the devastation, fell to her knees in the snow, her voice a mixture of hope and despair as she cried out, "Venus!"

Inside the collapsing pyramid, Venus and the monkey raced through the crumbling hallways. The walls were exploding around them, and the heat from the fires singed their fur. The monkey screamed, but he kept running, driven by Venus's telepathic encouragement.

As they neared the exit, the building gave one final, shuddering groan and began to collapse in earnest. With a last burst of energy, Venus and the monkey dove through the entrance they had created earlier. Just as the structure behind them imploded, sending a shockwave of dust and debris into the air.

They lay in the snow, Venus panting heavily and covered in soot, the remnants of the pyramid smoldering behind them. The sky above was filled with the aftermath of the explosion, and the violet pulse still lingered like an otherworldly beacon.

Evelyn, seeing Venus emerge from the wreckage, stumbled to her feet and ran towards her, tears streaming down her face. "Venus, you made it!" she cried, pulling the exhausted dog into a tight embrace.

The other Guardians gathered around, their expressions a mix of relief and awe.

As the dust settled and the sky cleared, the Guardians and the wolves formed a protective circle around Venus, their eyes filled with concern and questions. The monkey, still trembling but safe, climbed onto the Alpha wolf's back, holding on tightly.

"Venus, what happened in there?" Bjorn asked, his voice filled with worry and anticipation.

Venus barked, trying to convey the events, but without the magical necklace, her barks were just that—barks. Frustration and sadness filled her eyes as she realized she could no longer communicate directly with her friends. She felt the weight of Selene's sacrifice and the urgency to explain everything.

Then, Selene's last words echoed in her mind: "Use telepathy."

Taking a deep breath, Venus focused her thoughts and reached out to the Guardians telepathically. "Selene has sacrificed herself," she conveyed, her mental voice trembling with emotion. "She entered the network to destroy the magician's control from within. It was the only way."

The Guardians fell silent, absorbing her words. Sadness and respect for Selene washed over them. Lord Cedric bowed his head, his antlers glowing softly in the twilight. "She was a great warrior and a true leader," he said solemnly.

Bjorn, his voice choked with emotion, added, "Selene's bravery and sacrifice will not be forgotten. She gave everything to save us and the world."

Seraphina, in her pirate form, raised her silver goblet. "To Selene, a warrior with unmatched courage and honor," she said, her voice strong despite her grief. "May her spirit find peace and may we live up to the example she set."

The Guardians each took a drink from the pirate's goblet, passing it around the circle. Beatrice and Evelyn joined in, their eyes glistening with tears as they honored their fallen leader.

As the cup returned to Seraphina, the wolves began to howl, their mournful cries echoing through the snowy landscape. The sound was both a tribute and a farewell, filled with the raw emotion of their loss. Venus, feeling the deep connection with her pack and the pain of their shared sorrow, raised her head and joined in the howl.

The combined sound of wolves and Guardians filled the air, a poignant requiem for Selene and a promise to continue the fight she had begun. The sky seemed to shimmer in response, as if acknowledging the great sacrifice and the indomitable spirit of those left behind.

The battle was over, but the journey was far from complete.

Together, they would honor Selene's memory by continuing to protect the world from darkness, guided by her wisdom and courage.

As the Guardians and wolves finished their tribute to Selene, the world around them began to change. The battle against the magician and his hold over technology had been won,

but the real victory was unfolding far from the icy battlefield.

Chapter 12 – 'Evergreen Awakening'

As the echoes of the final battle faded into the snowy landscape, the Guardians, exhausted and grieving the loss of Selene, stood in somber silence. The distant hum of engines soon pierced the stillness, growing louder as a sleek space jet descended gracefully onto the battlefield. Its futuristic design cut through the snowy expanse, landing smoothly and opening its hatch to reveal a bustling scene of security personnel and a film crew, cameras already rolling.

From the jet emerged Eons, a man of striking presence. His sharp features and confident stride were unmistakable, marking him as the renowned social media mogul behind Cosmos, the influential network with a shining star emblem. Eons approached the group, his gaze sweeping over the aftermath before settling on Evelyn, Beatrice, and the remaining Guardians.

"I had to see it for myself," Eons said, his voice carrying a blend of authority and empathy. "My network, Cosmos, has been live streaming this battle. It was overtaken by the dark magician's forces. The chaos, the misinformation—it was out of control. None of my programmers could contain it."

He gestured toward his team and the film crew, who stood at the ready, their demeanor respectful yet purposeful. "I've brought them for protection and to start telling the world the truth. The people need to see what really happened here."

Evelyn stepped forward, her expression a mix of weariness and resolve. "Eons, what's your plan now? The world needs to know the truth."

Eons nodded, his face serious. "I'm committed to the truth. I'll ensure that your names are cleared. The world will know you as the heroes you are. Evelyn, Beatrice, the Guardians— you saved us all."

Turning to address the live audience through the cameras, Eons's voice resonated with conviction. "To everyone watching, you are witnessing the true heroes of our time. These brave individuals and their allies fought valiantly to save us from a darkness that threatened to consume everything. Their story is one of courage, sacrifice, and hope. The truth will be revealed."

He then glanced at Venus, who stood beside the monkey, the latter bouncing with excitement. "Venus, your bravery made a tremendous difference. We owe you much."

The monkey, sensing the positive attention, began doing somersaults, eliciting smiles from everyone present. The Guardians exchanged glances, their expressions reflecting a mixture of relief and sorrow. Bjorn stepped forward, his voice heavy with emotion. "We've accomplished our mission. But now, it's time for us to say goodbye."

Lord Cedric, now in his human form, nodded in agreement. "Our work here is done. The world must heal, and it is in capable hands."

As the wind picked up, swirling snow around the group, the Guardians bid farewell to Evelyn, Beatrice, and the wolves. The wolves howled a mournful tune, their voices echoing the gravity of their shared journey.

Eons, recognizing the significance of the moment, stepped forward with a gesture of gratitude. "As a token of thanks, I'd like to offer you a ride back to Evergreen. It's the least I can do for those who saved my network and, more importantly, our world."

Evelyn and Beatrice accepted the offer with gratitude. The wolves, ever loyal, moved closer, ready to board the jet. Venus and the monkey followed, with Eons expressing his deep appreciation to Venus. "Venus, your courage has given us all a second chance. I will make sure your story is told and remembered."

With the space jet prepared for departure, Eons led the way, his security team ensuring everyone's safe boarding. As the jet lifted off, ascending above the icy battlefield, it made its way toward the warmth and familiarity of Evergreen.

Inside the luxurious interior of the jet, Eons turned to Evelyn and Beatrice, the cameras still capturing every moment. "This is just the beginning of a new era. Thanks to your efforts, people are starting to see the world differently. They're waking up."

Evelyn smiled softly, her hand resting gently on Venus's head. "We've done what we could. Now it's up to everyone else to keep the change going."

The jet soared through the sky, carrying them back to Evergreen, where a new dawn awaited. The world had been given a chance to rediscover its beauty, connections, and truths. And with heroes like Evelyn, Beatrice, and the Guardians, there was hope that this new beginning would be embraced by all.

Back in Evergreen, the air was crisp, and the sky a brilliant blue. People who had once been glued to their screens now looked up and around, their faces reflecting a blend of confusion and wonder.

A young woman, previously engrossed in her social media feed, put her phone away and took a deep breath. She smiled as she noticed the vibrant colors of the flowers lining the park path, their petals swaying gently in the breeze. Nearby, an elderly man, who had been scrolling endlessly, looked up and struck up a conversation with a passerby, sharing a genuine laugh.

In a quaint café, couples who had been sitting in silence, absorbed in their devices, began to reconnect. A man put his phone down and reached across the table to take his partner's hand. "I love you," he said softly, and she smiled, her eyes meeting his for the first time in what felt like ages.

Bookstores and libraries, once quiet and nearly forgotten, began to buzz with life. People rediscovered the joy of holding a physical book, turning pages, and losing themselves in stories that didn't require a screen. The town's small bookshop saw children huddled around a storyteller, their faces alight with excitement and imagination.

The infamous "Yik Yokers," who had once danced for their online followers, paused and looked around. They began to see the world in a new light. The need for virtual validation faded, replaced by a newfound appreciation for the real world and its simple, yet profound beauty.

In parks, families played together without the distraction of notifications. Friends met and talked, really talked, sharing stories and dreams. The sense of community grew stronger, and with it, a deeper, more spiritual connection to life itself.

The grass swayed gently in the wind, and the flowers seemed to bloom brighter. The world itself appeared to have taken a breath, relieved of the constant digital hum that had overshadowed its natural beauty. People began to realize that life was not something to be experienced through a screen but to be lived fully and authentically.

Chapter 13 – 'Cottage Calm'

The quaint cottage nestled in the woods of Evergreen exuded an air of tranquility and renewal. Morning sunlight filtered through the dense canopy, casting a warm, golden hue across the yard. Inside, Beatrice, Evelyn, Venus, and the monkey sat together at the kitchen table, savoring a rare moment of peace after their grueling journey.

Evelyn carefully unfolded a newspaper, laying it out before them. The headline leaped out with an optimistic flair: "A New Dawn: The World Awakens to a Brighter Future." The accompanying article detailed the dramatic societal shift—people reconnecting with each other, rediscovering the natural world's beauty, and stepping away from their screens to embrace more meaningful, offline lives.

Beatrice looked up from the paper, her face bright with a mixture of wonder and satisfaction. "It's incredible, isn't it? We've truly made a difference. The world is changing for the better."

Evelyn's eyes sparkled with pride and relief as she nodded. "Selene's sacrifice was not in vain. We've helped people remember what truly matters."

Venus, now looking content, glanced out the open window where the wolves' silhouettes were visible in the forest. Their presence was a reassuring reminder of their shared history and the trials they had faced together.

The Alpha wolf emerged from the treeline, padding silently toward the cottage. He approached Venus with a wise and gentle gaze. "We will always be close by," he communicated telepathically, his voice resonant and deep. "If danger returns, so will we."

Venus nuzzled the Alpha through the open window, feeling the profound strength of their bond. The monkey, perched on a nearby chair, watched with wide, curious eyes, its tail flicking in anticipation.

The Alpha wolf delicately placed a new necklace around Venus's neck. The necklace was intricately designed, adorned with ancient runes and symbols that glowed softly with magical energy. "This is from the Guardians," the Alpha explained through telepathy. "If you ever need us in the future, you will know what to do."

Venus felt the weight of the necklace—a tangible reminder of the enduring bond between her and the Guardians. She barked softly, her gratitude evident in her expression.

Beatrice and Evelyn joined Venus, each placing a comforting hand on her back. Beatrice spoke gently, her voice filled with emotion. "We've faced so much together, and now we've given the world a chance to heal. Let's honor Selene's memory by living fully and protecting this peace."

Evelyn's eyes misted with unshed tears as she nodded in agreement. "We'll cherish every moment and be prepared for whatever comes next. We're stronger together."

The Alpha wolf bowed his head slightly, then turned and vanished back into the woods, followed by the other wolves. Though unseen, their presence would remain a comforting reminder of their vigilance.

As the morning light continued to bathe the forest in warmth, Venus, Beatrice, Evelyn, and the monkey remained at the cottage, their hearts buoyed by the newspaper's hopeful message. The world had indeed begun a new chapter, and they stood ready to embrace the future with hope and resilience, guided by the bonds they had forged and the mission they had fulfilled.

The necklace around Venus's neck glinted with a soft, magical glow, symbolizing their journey, their sacrifices, and the enduring power of their unity. As they gazed out over the serene woods, they knew that whatever challenges might arise, they would face them together—Guardians of a brighter, more connected world.

www.ingramcontent.com/pod-product-compliance
Lightning Source LLC
Chambersburg PA
CBHW072119300726
48975CB00003B/857